Augustus Jessopp

John Donne

Sometime Dean of St. Paul's - A.D. 1621-1631

Augustus Jessopp

John Donne
Sometime Dean of St. Paul's - A.D. 1621-1631

ISBN/EAN: 9783337402297

Printed in Europe, USA, Canada, Australia, Japan

Cover: Foto ©Andreas Hilbeck / pixelio.de

More available books at **www.hansebooks.com**

·JOHN DONNE·

SOMETIME DEAN OF ST. PAUL'S

A.D. 1621–1631

BY

AUGUSTUS JESSOPP, D.D.

RECTOR OF SCARNING

WITH TWO PORTRAITS

METHUEN & CO.

36 ESSEX STREET, W.C.

LONDON

1897

TO

MY GIFTED AND MUCH VALUED FRIEND

HENRY WILLETT

I OFFER THIS LITTLE VOLUME

A TRIBUTE OF LOYALTY AND

HIGH REGARD

PREFACE

IT is fifty years since, as an undergraduate at Cambridge, I projected and began to make collections for a complete edition of the works of Dr. Donne.

In those days there was a great revival of the study of our seventeenth-century divinity, the result of the great Oxford Movement. Young men were told that the great teachers of that period were the safest and the wisest guides to follow. Certainly we knew none better. The Textual Criticism of the New Testament was then in its infancy, and the New Theology was not yet born.

Perhaps it was just as well that publishers shrank from embarking in so ambitious a venture as I had contemplated; and soon circumstances intervened which took from me "the dream of doing and the other dream of done."

In 1855, however, I issued a reprint of Donne's little-known *Essays in Divinity*, with a brief account of the author's life. The critics said that the volume was absurdly overloaded with foolish notes and an unnecessary display of learning. I think the critics were right. When young men are in the happy

twenties, they are apt to "show off," especially if
they are solitary students; and I confess that to this
day, when I have occasion to look into the small pages
of that little bantling of mine, I feel as Mr. Pen-
dennis felt when recurring to one of his early reviews
—nothing astonished him so much as the erudition
which he found he had amassed in his first attempts
in criticism.

Since those days I have never quite given up my
old interest in the life and works of Dr. Donne. The
design of publishing a complete edition has long since
been abandoned; but the hope of issuing the life and
letters of the great Dean I still clung to, till the conviction forced itself upon me that there was one who
was better qualified for such a task than I could ever
hope to be.

I have never been able to feel much enthusiasm for
Donne as a poet; and it is as a poet that Donne's
fame has chiefly come down to us. Who was I that
I should undertake to deal with the life of the man
whose poetry I had not the power of appreciating at
its worth? There must be some deficiency, some
obliquity, in my own mind. It was only slowly and
reluctantly that I was brought to see that such a
work as I had hoped to do, only Mr. Edmund Gosse
was fitted to undertake. There is no man in England
who has written so exquisitely on Donne as he, or
shown such subtile sympathy with his poetic genius.
It is to him, accordingly, that I resign that delightful

and honourable task which I once hoped to accomplish myself. It is from him that any adequate and elaborate biography is to be looked for.

In the meantime, and while we are waiting for something better, I have been glad to draw up the following sketch, which I hope will be found trustworthy as far as it goes. I have dealt with Donne as one of the great *leaders of religion* in his time; it is from this point of view that the volume should be read.

There are two biographies in literature that can never be superseded: the *Life of Agricola* by Tacitus is one, Izaak Walton's *Life of Donne* is the other. Every incident which Tacitus mentions in the *Agricola* is probably narrated with strict accuracy: the same cannot be said of Walton's work. Tacitus was by nature and training a historian; Walton was a hero-worshipper, who could not help idealising his heroes. The age in which he lived was comparatively careless about unadorned historic fact. Devout people had not yet left off reading the lives of the saints *for edification*, and still expected a certain measure of panegyric at the hands of biographers. It is not to be wondered at if Walton's *Donne* should be full of mistakes in matters of detail. But it is a matchless work of art, which if you try to mend you can only spoil. To retouch it, to correct it, to edit it (as the phrase is), would be to smother it with learned dust and ashes. In our time we have substituted photography for portraiture; and so much more is known of Donne's life now than could have been known to Walton, that a new Life, setting forth the results of recent research, seems to be required.

If no authorities are cited for the new facts that have been brought forward, that is no fault of mine. I am told—and I suspect it is true—that the generality of readers would rather be without them. In literature as in the ordinary affairs of life we must be content to trust one another. If a man tries to cheat his neighbours by imposing upon their credulity, he will not long escape being found out. Of course, to err is human; but, for myself, I would not, for all that this world could give, pass into that other world— the world of spirits blest—fearing to meet my great teacher and master and friend, Dr. John Donne, as I should fear to meet him if consciously I had borne false witness here—against him or for him.

TABLE OF CONTENTS

THE LIFE OF JOHN DONNE

INTRODUCTION

WHEN it is said that "great men are the product of their age," what is meant to be conveyed by the phrase is that every man who plays a conspicuous part in the history of his own country or of the world—whether it be in politics, literature, or religion —must needs be influenced by his environment.

But this is more or less true of every man, and not only of the most gifted and the most famous. We cannot hope to estimate rightly the life-story of either the obscure or the most eminent in their genera-tion, till we know something of the days in which they lived, the events in which they took part, the people with whom they were brought into contact, or the influences that were exercised upon them during their career.

It is especially necessary that we should know something of these factors when we are setting our-selves to the serious study of a life which has come down to us as an exemplar life from an age and a state of society that has passed away. For in every age the greatest are they who assimilate most readily and most largely all those elements of intellectual and

I

spiritual nutrition, which contribute towards the
growth and building up of noble characters, but
which lower natures take little heed of, neglect and
run their dull course without regarding. Small men
remain small in the best times or the worst; the
great leaders of mankind more than keep pace with
the resistless wheels of the chariot of progress, because
they themselves are the charioteers.

All this is exemplified with curious emphasis in
the life of the man of genius who has been called the
Poet Preacher, Dr. John Donne, the great Dean of
St. Paul's.

On his father's side he was sprung from an ancient
Welsh stock,—a "Knightly Family," as the old writers
designated such landowners as could boast of a
succession of belted knights among their ancestors,—
the Dwnns of Dwynn in Radnorshire. Of this house,
John Donne the elder appears to have been a
younger son, and, according to the very common
practice of those times, he was early sent to London,
apprenticed to a London merchant, and in due course
was admitted to the freedom of the city, and enrolled
in the ancient Guild of Ironmongers. He exhibited
a great capacity for business, rapidly succeeded as a
merchant, and had already realised a considerable
fortune, when he died, while still young, in January
1576.

On his mother's side, Dr. Donne was descended
from the family of Sir Thomas More, whose judicial
murder, when he was Lord Chancellor of England, is
only too well known to us all.

1. He died for conscience' sake upon the scaffold
in 1536.

2. Elizabeth, a sister of Sir Thomas More, had married John Rastall, one of our early printers and a barrister of Lincoln's Inn. He too suffered much for his vehement opposition to the Reformation; he is said to have witnessed the barbarous execution of his brother-in-law, and he himself appears to have died in prison that same year. He too a sufferer for conscience' sake.

3. Margaret Griggs, another inmate of the house of Sir Thomas More, and a kinswoman and adopted daughter of the illustrious Chancellor, became the wife of Dr. John Clement about the year 1530. She died an exile for her faith, at Malines in 1570, and her husband, also an exile for conscience' sake, survived her two years, he too dying in the foreign land a confessor for the faith for which he suffered.

4. Winifred, the daughter of these two last-named persons, married William Rastall, the son of John Rastall mentioned above, who was Sir Thomas More's brother-in-law. William Rastall became one of the Judges of the Common Pleas. He too, under the pressure of the Elizabethan laws enforcing conformity upon all, abjured the realm for the second time in 1563. He ended his days at Louvain in 1565, and was buried there beside Winifred, his wife, who had died there ten years before. They were both exiles in the foreign land for conscience' sake, as so many of their kindred had been before them and after them.

5. Elizabeth, the daughter of William Rastall, the judge, and Winifred, his wife, married John Heywood, the epigrammatist. John Heywood narrowly escaped being hung by Henry VIII., was high in favour under Queen Mary, but at the accession of Queen Elizabeth

he felt himself compelled to retire to Malines, where he too died an exile. There was no place for men of his opinions in his native land.

6. John Heywood had by his wife Elizabeth (Rastall) three children—two sons and a daughter. The sons were Jasper and Ellis Heywood, two of the most staunch and aggressive supporters of the Roman creed and ritual of their time, and two of the first Englishmen admitted to the Society of Jesus. They too were banished the realm and died in exile. Let us not grudge them, too, the credit of having died far away from home for conscience' sake.

7. The sister of these two eminent brothers was the mother of Dr. Donne. She was notorious as a "stubborn Papist" all her life. She is said to have been seriously despoiled of her substance for her non-conformity, though she lived long enough to see the cruel laws of the previous reign greatly relaxed by the more tolerant lenity of James I. But as she had lived, so she died in conscientious communion with the Church of Rome.

8. To this long and miserable catalogue of sufferers for their faith, sufferers to whom we cannot deny the merit of sincerity and a certain measure of heroism —though their beliefs were not as ours are, and though we may assert with firm insistence that they were on the wrong side, the side of error—one more name must be added.

In May 1593 a Roman priest named William Harrington was arrested in Thavies Inn—one of the Inns of Law in Holborn—at the chambers of Donne's younger brother, Henry, who thereupon was committed to the Clink Prison for the crime of concealing the proscribed Seminarist. A few weeks later young Henry Donne (he was hardly nineteen) caught jail fever, and died in the prison.

Thus it appears that, during four generations, at least five blood relations of Donne had suffered cruelly in their persons or their estates for what they believed to be the true faith of a Christian. Well might he say, in his preface to the *Pseudo Martyr*, written in 1610, "No family (which is not of far larger extent and greater branches) hath endured and suffered more in their persons and fortunes for obeying the teachers of Roman doctrine." . . . "I had a larger work to do than many other men," he adds, "for I was first to blot out certain impressions of the Roman religion and to wrestle both against the examples and against the reasons, by which some hold was taken, and some anticipations early laid upon my conscience, both by persons who by nature had a power and superiority over my will, and others who, by their learning and good life, seemed to me justly to claim an interest, for the guiding and rectifying of mine understanding in these matters."

Three years before John Donne was born, the Bull of Pope Pius v., proclaiming the excommunication of Queen Elizabeth, was nailed to the door of the Bishop of London's Palace during the night of the 15th May 1570. Next year the Legislature answered this challenge by making it penal for any priest of the Roman communion to absolve or reconcile any of Her Majesty's subjects, or exercise any priestly functions in the realm. On the face of these enactments, it was no longer possible for any subjects of the Queen to halt between two opinions in matters of religion.

Everybody's hand was forced, so to speak; everyone
had to take his stand on the pope's side as a
"Catholic," or on the queen's side as a "Heretic,"
or Anglican, which in those days was declared to
mean the same thing. Religious toleration in the
sixteenth century was hardly dreamt of as a political
possibility, and the tactics of the popes and their
more fiery and zealous advisers all went in the
direction of making freedom of thought and freedom
of opinion impossible. People had not yet learnt to
think for themselves; for generations they had been
kept in leading strings; and during the first twenty
years of Elizabeth's reign the great majority of
educated Englishmen were accustomed to and were
more or less attached to the ancient ritual, and
would have been glad to see it restored with its old
pomp and splendour.

Meanwhile, the course of events at home, and
more especially abroad, were very powerfully in-
fluencing the feelings and opinions and prejudices of
the great bulk of the nation, arousing in men's minds
a sturdier and more passionate patriotism, an increasing hatred of French cruelty, Spanish ferocity,
Italian guile; awakening a spirit of adventure and a
desire to travel into distant lands, while the growth of
our trade and commerce had made the lust of wealth
become more absorbing and restless than it had been
among us probably since the fourteenth century.

We have only to remember that in the year 1572
the Dutch Republic was founded, Sir Francis Drake
sailed to Panama, and then first "stared at the
Pacific." In that year, too, the atrocious Massacre of
St. Bartholomew's Day shocked and horrified the world,

and the only remaining English duke, Thomas Howard, suffered upon the scaffold for what was commonly believed to be an attempt at rebellion—fomented by the pope, and suggested by the King of Spain. It was an Annus Mirabilis indeed, the year before John Donne was born.

CHAPTER I

EARLY LIFE

JOHN DONNE was born in the parish of St. Nicholas Olave, London, some time in the year 1573.

His father, John Donne the elder, served his apprenticeship to Mr. James Harvey, afterwards Sir James, and Alderman of London. Mr. Donne was himself admitted to the freedom of the City some time in the reign of Queen Mary, and in 1559 he was managing the business of a rich widow, Mrs. Anne or Agnes Lewen, being at that time a member of the Ironmongers' Company. Her husband, Thomas Lewen, had died in 1557, and died childless. By his will, dated 20th April 1555, he bequeathed all his property in London and Bucks, which was very considerable, to his widow for her life, and after her death he directed that it should pass to the Master, Warden, and Company of "the mystery or occupation" of the Ironmongers of the city of London and their successors, to hold the same *until such time as a new monastery be erected at Sawtrey, in the county of Huntingdon, of the same order of monks as were then in the old monastery before its suppression*, charged with the maintenance of a mass priest in the Church of St. Nicholas aforesaid, to pray and preach therein, and prepare other services as set out. . . . The said

8

master and wardens are further enjoined to pay yearly to the Friars Observants within the realm of England the sum of five pounds; and a like sum to two poor scholars, one to be of Oxford and the other at Cambridge, towards their maintenance. . . . Immediately after the rebuilding of a monastery at Sawtrey, the said master and wardens are to pay to the abbot or prior the money previously devoted to the mass priest . . . and shall cause a mass daily to be said, and four sermons yearly to be preached, within the said monastery for the good of his soul.

As far as I know, this is the first and last important bequest made after the plunder of the monasteries by Henry VIII. for the restoration of a suppressed religious house; and as the widow did not die till the 26th October 1562, when Queen Elizabeth had been on the throne nearly four years. Alderman Lewen's intentions, so far as the rebuilding of this Cistercian abbey was concerned, were never carried into effect, and the bulk of the property is still held, I believe, by the Ironmongers' Company, subject only to the charges for maintaining the two scholars at Oxford and Cambridge down to the present time.

Mrs. Lewen made her own will in January 1559-60, appointing her servant, John Donne, now free of the said company, "one of her executors," and she bequeathed to him some very substantial legacies, including the " great messuage, with a garden attached," in which he resided at the time of his death, and where it appears that all his children were born. The house was destroyed during the fire of London in 1666.

Mr. Donne served the office of warden to the Company in 1574; but while still in the prime of life he died early in 1576, leaving his widow with a large fortune, and an ample provision for each of his six children. Three of these children died in infancy. The shares of these three thereupon went to increase the portions of the two surviving brothers. A sister, who received her portion, lived on till the year 1616, as we shall hear later on.

By the untimely death of young Henry Donne, a few weeks before he came of age, all the accumulated wealth intended to be divided among five devolved upon the surviving son, John, before he had completed his twenty-third year.

The two boys were brought up under a private tutor in their mother's house, and were educated with great care; but they were strictly trained according to the proscribed tenets of the Church of Rome. As children it was inevitable that they should be greatly influenced by their uncle, Jasper Heywood, the Jesuit Father, who, from 1581 till 1584, "was esteemed the Provincial of the English Jesuits," and gave himself the airs of a legate from the apostolic see, even going so far as to summon a Provincial Council, which resulted in working much mischief, and eventually occasioned the banishment of Father Heywood himself, together with that of some seventy other priests, whom it was not thought advisable to deal with according to the full rigour of the law. Father Heywood was a prisoner in the Tower of London during the greater part of 1584, and by some special favour, which remains unexplained, " he was permitted to receive visits from his sister, who was able to bestow upon him some care and nursing." That sister was

Donne's mother, and it is fair to conjecture that during some of those visits she may have been attended by her son, already then a boy of conspicuous promise, "with a good command both of the French and Latin tongue." It was probably, too, at the suggestion and advice of their astute and very learned uncle (himself at one time a Fellow of All Souls College) that the two brothers, John and Henry Donne, the one in his twelfth, the other in his eleventh year, were entered at Hart Hall, in the University of Oxford, on the 23rd October 1584—two or three months before Father Heywood was sent out of the country, never to return.

It seems to have been part of Jasper Heywood's policy to induce the *Catholic* gentry to send their sons to the English universities as early as possible, that is, as soon as they could be admitted to matriculate. The object was to give the lads the advantage of a university training and familiarity with English academic life before the oath of allegiance could be administered to them. That oath had been worded so as to be especially offensive to the Romanists; but it was not exacted from any before the age of sixteen. Accordingly, between 1581 and 1584, eighteen of these boys under fourteen were matriculated at Oxford, and among them were the two brothers with whom we are concerned.

Six months before Donne came into residence, Sir Henry Wotton, then a youth of fifteen, had come up from Winchester, and entered at New College; but, either because there was no room for him there, or because he preferred the society elsewhere, he removed to Hart Hall, and thus the lifelong friendship between him and Donne began. | Neither Wotton nor Donne appear to have taken a degree at Oxford. Wotton certainly, and Donne almost as certainly, left Oxford, and spent the next few years in foreign travel, each / probably with the view of acquiring that knowledge of foreign languages in which they became proficient, and so fitting themselves for the diplomatic service (as we should say nowadays) of which Wotton became a distinguished ornament, and in which Donne again and again endeavoured, but fruitlessly, to find a career.

During these years of travel he disappears from our view, but turns up again in 1592, when on the 6th May he entered at Lincoln's Inn, occupying the same chambers with Christopher Brooke — a prominent member of a remarkable band of poets and men of letters, the intellectual leaders of this brilliant period of English literature.

It seems that a select society, which numbered among its members almost all the most gifted *wits* who were the ornaments of Queen Elizabeth's court, used to assemble at the Mermaid Tavern in Bread Street, on the first Friday in every month, to enjoy a convivial meeting. The gatherings continued to be held for several years, and there are frequent allusions to the proceedings of this famous club in the light literature of the time. At the Mermaid there were wont to assemble such men as John Selden, Inigo Jones, Michael Drayton, John Hoskins, Ben Jonson, and many another, illustrious as poets, artists, or scholars, and others who rose to eminence as lawyers, or played no mean part in the politics of the country. Shakespeare himself was a member of the club, and frequently attended the meetings; there Donne appears to have formed some of the friendships which lasted through his life. In Francis Beaumont's well-known letter to Ben Jonson, the poet writes as follows of these meetings :—

> "What things have we seen
> Done at the Mermaid! heard words that have been
> So nimble and so full of subtle flame,
> As if that everyone from whence they came
> Had meant to put his whole wit in a jest,
> And had resolved to live a fool the rest
> Of his dull life; then when there hath been thrown
> Wit able enough to justify the town
> For three days past; with that might warrant be
> For the whole city to talk foolishly
> Till that were cancelled."

Fuller's famous description of the "wit combats" between Shakespeare and Ben Jonson [1] need hardly be quoted here.

Donne soon gained for himself a wide reputation, and, while pursuing his legal studies at Lincoln's Inn, he became a literary celebrity in London. His graceful person,[2] vivacity of conversation, and many accomplishments secured for him the *entrée* at the houses of the nobility and a recognised position among the celebrities of Queen Elizabeth's court. He was conspicuous as a young man of fortune who spent his money freely, and mixed on equal terms with the courtiers, and probably had the character of being richer than he was.

The tragical end of his brother Henry could not

---

[1] *Worthies of Warwickshire under Shakespeare.*

[2] "Dr. Donne, . . . a laureate wit; neither was it impossible that a vulgar soul should dwell in such promising features."—Hacket's *Life of the Lord Keeper Williams,* § 74.

but have been a great shock to him, but even that
calamity resulted in a material addition to his
patrimony. On the other hand, his close connection
with the proscribed Recusants acted to some extent
to his discredit, and we know that at the time of his
marriage he lay under some suspicion of being still
tainted with sympathy with the Romanists and of
being less than loyal towards the Anglican creed and
ritual. He himself strongly protested against these
insinuations, but they were repeated nevertheless, and
doubtless they stood in the way of his advancement
at this period.

Walton says that "*about his nineteenth year*" Donne
"began seriously to survey and consider the body of
divinity as it was then controverted between the
Reformed and the Roman Church. . . . Being to
undertake this search, he believed the Cardinal
Bellarmine to be the best defender of the Roman
cause, and therefore betook himself to the examination of his reasons. The cause was weighty; and
wilful delays had been inexcusable both towards God
and his own conscience; he therefore proceeded in
this search with all moderate haste, and about the
twentieth year of his age did show the Dean of
Gloucester (Dr. Anthony Rudde) all the Cardinal's
works marked with many weighty observations under
his own hand; which works were bequeathed by him
at his death, as a legacy to a most dear friend."[1]

The disastrous termination of the last expedition

---

[1] Walton was careless in his chronology, and he has antedated this
period of study by at least two years. It is certain that Donne's study
of Bellarmine extended no further, at this time, than to the reading of

to the West Indies and the Spanish Main in 1595, under Drake and Hawkins, and the continued rumours of plots against the queen's life, which were believed to have had their origin at the court of Philip II., led to the conviction, which was very widely prevalent in England, that some blow should be struck at Spain, which might cripple her commerce, and be delivered nearer home than on the other side of the Atlantic. A secret expedition on a large scale was organised accordingly; and a fleet of a hundred and fifty sail, with twenty-two Dutch ships and seven thousand soldiers, set out in June 1596, with Lord Howard of Effingham as Lord High Admiral, and Robert, Earl of Essex, then in his twenty-ninth year, as General of the land forces. The admiral's flag was hoisted on board the *Ark*. Sir George Carew commanded the *Mary Rose*, Sir Francis Vere the *Rainbow*, Sir Walter Raleigh the *Warspite*, Sir Robert Southwell the *Lion*.

Not since the coming of the "Great Armada," eight years before, had such enthusiasm been aroused among the nobility, or so splendid a gathering been seen of young men of family eager to gain experience in war, and, if it might be so, distinction in fighting the Spaniard. The Lord Admiral was the veteran hero who had commanded the fleet in 1588. He was sailing in the very ship on board which he

the famous three volumes entitled *Disputationes de controversiis fidei adversus hujus temporis Hæreticos*, which were published in Lyons in 1593, and it is probable that he was moved to throw himself into the study of controversial divinity, not only by the appearance of this memorable work, which created a great sensation over all Europe, but by the profound impression which his brother's death must have produced upon his mind.

had dashed into the middle of the Armada off
Portland on the 22nd July: he was now sixty years old.
Sir Robert Southwell had married a daughter of Lord
Howard of *Effingham, and had been rear-admiral under
his father-in-law in the memorable year of victory.
George Carew had served for years in Ireland, and was
now Lieut.-General of the Ordnance. Sir Francis
Vere had fought under Leicester in the Low Countries,
though his chief laurels were yet to win. Sir Walter
Raleigh, twelve years before, had crossed the Atlantic,
and founded the settlement of Virginia; he too had
been one of the heroes of the '88; but his ship,
the *Warspite*—a vessel of eight hundred tons—had
been launched only three months before this new
expedition set sail. Under leaders such as these, it
was no wonder that every youth of spirit was burning
with the desire to take part in the adventure.
Knights and gentlemen, with their followers amount-
ing to nine hundred in number, were glad to serve as
volunteers, and among the first who offered himself
was young Donne. We are told that " he waited
upon the Earl of Essex," and was at once accepted. It
may be that he had already received an introduction to
the great man, whose younger brother, Walter Devereux,
had entered at Christ Church a term before he
himself had matriculated at Hart Hall, and who
probably had been among his Oxford friends.

Among the other chivalrous spirits on board the
admiral's ship in the Cadiz expedition, not the least
conspicuous of Donne's shipmates were young Thomas
Egerton and Francis Wooley of Pyrford in Surrey,
respectively the son and stepson of Sir Thomas
Egerton, afterwards Lord Ellesmere, who had been

made Keeper of the Great Seal and Lord High Chancellor a month before the fleet set sail. Between these young men and Donne it was inevitable that a friendship should spring up which stood the latter in good stead.

The Cadiz voyage had so brilliant a termination that it led to the fitting out of another expedition next year, which proved a disastrous failure. Donne, we are told, "was an eye-witness of those happy and unhappy employments"; he does not appear to have distinguished himself in the fighting, but the Lord Keeper's son was among those who were knighted for their gallantry. The fleet got back in October 1597, and immediately on his return to England Donne was appointed secretary to the Lord Keeper, " by the favour which your good son's love to me obtained," he says, when writing to his patron four years later. The secretaryship to the most exalted functionary in the realm was a position which any young man might have been proud to attain to in his twenty-third year, and a position, too, which afforded a prospect of "some more weighty employment in the state; for which his lordship did often protest he thought him very fit."

Donne's foot was now upon the ladder; a great career was before him. Living "in that fierce light which beats about a throne," he was brought into close relations with the most illustrious personages in the realm,—admitted to familiar and confidential intercourse with the great ones who were making history,— and winning the notice and admiration of people of wealth and high station, who proved themselves in the aftertime ready and eager to promote his advancement.

2

The young man, among his other gifts, had the great
advantage of being able to do with very little sleep.
He could read all night and be gay and wakeful and
alert all day.   He threw himself into the amusements
and frivolities of the court with all the glee of youth,
but never so as to interfere with his duties.   The
favourite of fortune, he was too the favourite of the
fortunate—the envy of some, he was the darling of
more.   Those of his contemporaries who knew him
intimately speak of him at all times as if there was
none like him; the charm of his person and manners
were irresistible.   He must have had much love to give,
or he could never have had so much bestowed upon him.
/ During these four years Donne's reputation as a
poet and wit was steadily increasing.   In the later
years of Elizabeth's reign there was a great deal of
literary activity, which was rather in danger of de-
generating into frivolity and affectation than rising to
seriousness.   People were happy and gay, and their
gaiety expressed itself in playfulness of style—in
songs and epigrams, in eccentricities of manner, in
far-fetched metaphors and odd fancies.   There was a
continual striving for effect—a taste for the fantastic,
which by no means discouraged obscurity in diction,
when the substance was often subordinated to the form,
and the thought wrapped up in verbiage, which sometimes rather concealed than expressed it in harmonious
language.   Donne, in his earlier writings, may be said
to have fallen into the sins of his time.   He wrote
much in verse — sonnets, lyrics, love-songs, elegies,
and satires.   In prose he threw off what he called his
" paradoxes " and problems—short essays, each containing some odd fancy or whimsical theory; as, " That

Nature is our worst Guide," "That all things kill
Themselves," "Why doth not Gold soil the Fingers?"
or "Why do Women delight much in Feathers?"
Ben Jonson, though he admired his cleverness, was
more than ordinarily severe upon him for his ruggedness. Why should subtlety of thought excuse neglect
of rhythm? Nevertheless, the young poet became
the rage, and his writings were widely circulated.
It was not the fashion to print such trifles; they were
handed about in manuscript, discussed at the ordinaries,
read out in clubs and coteries—the writers looking for
their reward in the shape of favours from those to
whom they were first presented or addressed, and not
infrequently in the shape of actual pecuniary honor-
arium. Very few of Donne's poems of this period
were published during his lifetime, and many which
are attributed to him and were issued under his name
never came from his hand. The carelessness with
which they were tossed into the lap of the public by
his unworthy son has rendered it almost a hopeless
task to distinguish between what is spurious and what
is genuine. Taking them, however, as we find them,
—if we except some few exquisite passages, which
will be remembered and quoted as long as our
language and literature live,—it is difficult to believe
that these earlier poems were not loved for the poet's
sake rather than the poet for the sake of his verse.

Meanwhile, though Donne was giving out a great
deal, he was taking in a great deal more. He himself confesses to "an hydroptic immoderate desire of
human-learning," which, in one of his poems, he calls
the "sacred hunger of science." He was so large
a buyer of books that their cost made no inconsider-

able drain upon his estate; and his reading embraced an extraordinary range of learning, which his command of foreign languages and his great versatility tempted him to widen. He read with his pen in his hand; annotating, digesting, commenting. Nothing came amiss: scholastic theology and casuistry, civil and common law, history, poetry, philosophy, even medicine; and all these subjects studied not only in the language of the learned, but in the vernacular of France, Italy, and Spain.

About the time that Donne had set sail on the Cadiz voyage in 1596, the Lord Keeper Egerton had married, as his second wife, Elizabeth, the widow of Sir John Wooley of Pyrford in Surrey, a sister of Sir George More of Losely, in the same county. Sir George was lieutenant of the town—a proud and ambitious man, pompous, choleric, and fond of making speeches, which he did very badly. He had at this time an unmarried daughter, a young lady now in her sixteenth year, whom it appears her aunt, Lady Egerton, on removing to York House, took with her as a companion. Her son, Francis Wooley, seems also to have resided with his stepfather, and the two young people may reasonably be supposed to have been intended for one another, according to the matchmaking custom of the time. But it seems they grew up rather as brother and sister; and however desirable an alliance between the heir of Pyrford and the daughter of Sir George More might have appeared to the latter, such an arrangement was probably never seriously entertained by the young man himself. Meanwhile, Ann More and Donne were necessarily thrown much together. The young lady developed

rapidly, and in her budding womanhood she had
constantly at her side the poet secretary, just ten
years her senior, in the bloom and beauty of his
youth, the peerless universal genius, whom to look at
and to listen to was to love. What else could follow
but that between the two an absorbing passion should
spring up? which soon got the mastery of both one
and the other, till considerations of prudence, even of
duty, exercised over them no restraining force. However much Sir George More may have expected that
Sir Francis Wooley would sooner or later marry his
daughter,—though the marriage of first cousins was at
this time looked upon as almost more than undesir-
able,—yet, as I have said, the young man had no
thought of marriage. He went up to Oxford and
took his degree in the spring of 1599; set up an
establishment at Pyrford shortly after; and in October
1601, young as he was, he entered Parliament as
member for the borough of Haslemere. He died un-
wedded in 1610.

Meanwhile, a great sorrow fell upon the Lord
Keeper's family. Donne's other close friend in the
Cadiz voyage, Sir Thomas Egerton, the Lord Keeper's
eldest son, was killed in Ireland in August 1599;
and five months later, January 1600, Lady Egerton
herself was carried to her grave. Over the great
house a gloom had come. From one passage in an
early letter of Donne's to Sir George More, it looks
as if his daughter Ann still continued for a while to
reside at York House, probably till the Lord Keeper
married his third wife, at the close of the year 1601.
If this were so, Sir George had really no one to
blame so much as himself for the culpable imprudence

of leaving a young girl—by this time a young woman
of eighteen—in daily and hourly communication with
a susceptible young man of extraordinary personal
attraction and many great gifts, and occupying a
position which quite justified him in dreaming of a
noble alliance. But when rumours and whisperings
of what was going on came to Sir George's ears—
all too late—the fond and ambitious father was
greatly incensed. He appears to have behaved with
insulting contempt to young Donne, treating the proposal of any marriage between the lovers as a thing
not to be heard of. He sent for his daughter to
Losely, and forbade all intercourse between the two.
Things, however, had gone too far. It was impossible
to prevent all intercourse between the young people.
The secretary must be in constant attendance upon
the Lord Keeper, the Chancellor of the Garter could
not keep his daughter away from all court entertainments. The lovers, even without intending it, would
be thrown together from time to time; and in more
than one of his poems, Donne makes mention of their
secret interviews. If we may take the fourth elegy
as a recital of facts, we must infer that Sir George
More had distinctly refused to sanction any marriage,
and that he had threatened to disinherit his daughter
if she and young Donne were seen together.

When the Parliament met in October 1601, Sir
George was compelled to be much in London, and his
daughter was with him. The dissolution took place
on the 19th December; and in the natural course of
things such meetings as had been contrived would
come to an end when Sir George and his family
returned for the winter to Losely. The lovers could

bear it no longer. First, they plighted their troth to
one another in a solemn contract, and, as it seems, in
the presence of witnesses; and almost immediately
afterwards they were married. Then they separated,
the bride returning to her father's house.

Perhaps what helped to precipitate matters was the
fear lest the young lady might be compelled against
her will to marry some more eligible suitor. Such
an arrangement was not uncommon at this time, when
a daughter's hand was assumed to be almost absolutely
at the disposal of her father, who could give her to
whom he pleased.

The clandestine marriage could not be kept secret
for long. Where it was celebrated we are not told.
Only two witnesses are known to have been present:
Christopher Brooke, the rising young barrister, who
shared Donne's chambers with him in Lincoln's Inn,
gave the bride away, and his brother Samuel Brooke,
destined to become eventually Master of Trinity
College, Cambridge, performed the marriage ceremony.

A double offence had been committed by the parties
concerned. First, an offence against the Canon Law
in marrying a girl without the consent of her father;
and secondly, the civil offence against the Common
Law.[1] It was a very serious business. It became
plain that a disclosure must be made; the only
question remaining was—who should act as mediator
between the bridegroom and his father-in-law?

On the last day of January or on the first of
February 1602, Henry Percy, Earl of Northumberland, one of the wealthiest and most powerful noblemen

[1] See *Treatise on the Laws relating to Infants*, by W. Macpherson
of the Inner Temple, London, 1847.

in England, undertook the delicate office; the tidings brought immeasurable provocation and dismay to Sir George More; he was furious, there were no bounds to his expressions of indignation; he would never be reconciled to his daughter, never forgive the perfidious husband who had beguiled her; he would set the law in its utmost rigour to bring down vengeance upon all concerned in the nefarious business, nor would he hear of excuse, palliation, or pardon. On the 2nd February, Donne, who seems to have been suffering from one of his serious attacks of illness, addressed a letter to Sir George from his chambers in the Savoy, giving a full account of the business, making a very humble confession of his fault, but beseeching his father-in-law "so to deal in it as the persuasions of nature, reason, wisdom, and Christianity shall inform you, and to accept the words of one whom you may now raise or scatter, which are, that as my love is directed unchangeably upon her, so all my labours shall concur to her contentment and to show my humble obedience to youself."

So far from this letter producing any good effect, nothing would serve but that the law should be set in motion without delay. Donne was committed to the Fleet Prison, Christopher Brooke was sent to the Marshalsea, and his brother to some other place of confinement. But what was worst of all was, that Sir George had peremptorily demanded that the Lord Keeper should dismiss his secretary; and dismissed he was. Meanwhile, the young bride was kept in strict confinement in her father's house at Losely, suffering acutely from anxiety and grief; her husband, who was now lying very ill in his chambers, was forbidden to

communicate with her, and she was not spared the
hearing of certain abominable stories circulated and
repeated to her husband's discredit. Matters mended
very slowly. The pair were kept separate till the
High Commission Court should adjudicate upon the
cause that had been brought before it, and in the
meanwhile Donne was thrown entirely upon his own
resources and put to a great deal of expense in various
ways. Little by little, however, Sir George More got
to see the necessity of making the best of a bad
business. He began to relent when he found that
his son-in-law was *not* a mere adventurer in debt and
with little or no fortune, as he had been represented
to be. But such was the state of the law at this
time, so complicated by precedents and entanglements,
that it was not till the 27th April 1602 that the
marriage was confirmed by the Ecclesiastical Court,
and the pair were allowed to come together. By this
time Sir George More had repented of his folly and
obstinacy, and had got to see that Donne was not so
unworthy of his daughter's hand as he had assumed
him to be, in the first violence of his exasperation;
and he even went so far as to ask the Lord Keeper
to reinstate his late secretary in his office. It was,
however, one thing for the Lord Keeper to dismiss
his secretary at the instance of his importunate and
choleric brother-in-law, and quite another to reappoint
him when that brother-in-law had come to his senses
and to a better mind. Lord Egerton replied with
much dignity that he had " parted with a friend and
such a secretary as was fitter to serve a king than a
subject, yet that, though he was unfeignedly sorry for
what he had done, it was inconsistent with his place

and credit to discharge and readmit servants at the request of passionate petitioners."

Donne had won his wife, but the question now was how he should maintain her? Sir George, though professing to be reconciled to the marriage, still refused to give his daughter any marriage portion, or make any settlement upon her; and it seems that he continued obdurate for a year or so, probably till the birth of the first child, early in 1603. Then he agreed to make an allowance equivalent to about £500 a year of our money. With this, and the remains of Donne's own fortune, which evidently was by no means all spent, the young couple could hardly be considered in very straitened circumstances, even though they had been brought up in affluence. At this point, however, a friend intervened with substantial assistance. As the Lord Keeper's son had been the means of introducing Donne to his father and of getting for him his place as secretary, so now his stepson came forward nobly and showed his regard for his former companion-in-arms. Mr. Francis Wooley was not only the Lord Chancellor's stepson, but he was the nephew of Sir George More. Mr. Wooley had inherited at the death of his father, Sir John, Latin Secretary to Queen Elizabeth and one of the Privy Council, a splendid estate at Pyrford in Surrey, about six miles from Guildford. The mansion was a very magnificent one, surrounded by a large park well stocked with deer, and twice during her reign Queen Elizabeth had been sumptuously entertained there. Young Francis Wooley was still under age at the time of Donne's marriage, but, on the decree being pronounced, and the bride having been restored to her

husband, Mr. Wooley at once offered the young couple
an asylum at Pyrford, and here they were invited to
make their home. The invitation was accepted, and
at Pyrford, Donne, his wife, and at least one child,
remained for the next year or two. It is almost
certain that they were living here at the death of
Queen Elizabeth, on the 24th March 1603, and that
they were still residing with Sir Francis (who was
knighted at the Charter House on the 11th May)
when James I. paid a state visit to his mansion on
the 10th August, passing on next day to Sir George
More's famous seat at Losely. At the new court
there were many changes going on, and a new chance
of a career was offered to an accomplished young man
with many friends; but it was absolutely necessary
that an aspirant for court favour should be in constant
attendance, and Donne's friends strongly urged upon
him the advisability of removing to London. He saw
the prudence of the advice, and early in 1605 he hired
a house at Micham in Surrey, then a favourite place of
residence for Londoners of large means and position.
Sir Nicholas Throckmorton Carew, who had married
another daughter of Sir George More, was Lord of
the Manor of Micham; Sir Thomas Grymes, another
brother-in-law, lived hard by at Camberwell; and
Sir Julius Cæsar, Master of the Rolls, and a great
friend of Donne's, had a splendid house in the parish,
where Queen Elizabeth had been entertained in
September 1598. Thus Donne was among his friends
and connections. At Micham he continued to reside
for at least five years; during which time five of his
children were born, four of whose names are to be
found in the register of baptisms of the parish. Mean-

while, he had taken a lodging for himself in the
Strand that he might be near Whitehall. He was
warmly welcomed by his old friends and by many of
the nobility and people of influence and position, who
hoped to further the young man's interest, while, as
the fashion was, they acted the part of patrons by
giving him from time to time substantial assistance.
But as for any preferment, none came.

> "He waited, and learned waiting . . .
>   Spending youth in splendid lacquey work,
>   And famished with the emptiness of hope."

APPENDIX TO CHAPTER I

In no department of literature is the diversity of the style and language of the writers of the nineteenth and of the seventeenth century more strongly marked than in the letters of courtesy and friendship of the two periods respectively. Even the most cordial and affectionate letters of the earlier time appear to us so stilted and artificial that we find it hard to believe the writers were sincere in their expressions, or were not playing a part. The obscurity and the pedantry, as they appear to us, are irritating to modern readers. We cannot understand why men should have wrapped up their meaning in such involved sentences, or been content to say what they had to say in language so obscure and so unrhythmical. Yet, long before Donne had made for himself a reputation as a theologian and preacher, he had got to be regarded as one of the great letter-writers of his time. There is, even now, a curious fascination about his letters for those who have once become in touch and sympathy with the writer; but, as Donne can never be the poet of the many, so as a letter-writer, I think, he can be attractive *at first reading* only to the few. Nevertheless, I think it only fair to him, at this point in his biography, to give the reader some

example of his epistolary style, and in doing so I
have thought fit to furnish a brief selection from such
of his letters as are more or less autobiographical, and
the rather, because several of these are known but to
few, and are only accessible in volumes which are
scarce or rarely met with in private libraries.

The earliest letters of Donne's which have come
down to us are those which give us some curious
information regarding his marriage. The first was
evidently the letter which gave the earliest intelligence
to Sir George More of what had happened six weeks
before, and was not improbably delivered by the Earl
of Northumberland. Donne seems to have been very
ill at the time he sent the letter, but this did not
prevent his being at once thrown into the Fleet
Prison. From thence he was removed to the Marshalsea a fortnight later, and set at liberty upon his own
recognisances a few days later. These letters were
first published in 1835, and have never been reprinted
till now.

I.

[JOHN DONNE *to* SIR GEORGE MORE of Losely
House, Surrey, *2nd February* 1602.]

" SIR,—If a very respective fear of your displeasure,
and a doubt that my lord (whom I know, out of
your worthiness, to love you much) would be so
compassionate with you as to add his anger to yours,
did not so much increase my sickness as that I
cannot stir, I had taken the boldness to have done
the office of this letter by waiting upon you myself
to have given you truth and clearness of this matter

between your daughter and me, and to show you plainly the limits of our fault, by which I know you will proportion the punishment.

" So long since as her being at York House this had foundation, and so much then of promise and contract built upon it as, without violence to conscience, might not be shaken.

" At her lying in town this Parliament, I found means to see her twice or thrice. We both knew the obligation that lay upon us, and we adventured equally; and about three weeks before Christmas we married. And as at the doing there were not used above five persons, of which I protest to you by my salvation, there was not one that had any dependence or relation to you, so in all the passage of it did I forbear to use any such person, who by furtherance of it might violate any trust or duty towards you.

" The reasons why I did not foreacquaint you with it (to deal with the same plainness I have used) were these :—I knew my present estate less than fit for her. I knew (yet I knew not why) that I stood not right in your opinion. I knew that to have given any intimation of it had been to impossibilitate the whole matter. And then, having these honest purposes in our hearts and these fetters in our consciences, methinks we should be pardoned, if our fault be but this, that we did not, by forerevealing of it, consent to our hindrance and torment.

" Sir, I acknowledge my fault to be so great, as I dare scarce offer any other prayer to you in mine own behalf than this, to believe that I neither had dishonest end nor means. But for her, whom I tender much more than my fortunes or life (else I would, I might neither joy in this life nor enjoy the next), I humbly beg of you that she may not, to her danger, feel the terror of your sudden anger.

"I know this letter shall find you full of passion; but I know no passion can alter your reason and wisdom, to which I adventure to commend these particulars; that it is irremediably done; that if you incense, my lord, you destroy her and me; that it is easy to give us happiness, and that my endeavours and industry, if it please you to prosper them, may soon make me somewhat worthier of her.

"If any take the advantage of your displeasure against me, and fill you with ill thoughts of me, my comfort is that you know that faith and thanks are due to them only that speak when their informations might do good. . . .

"Sir, I have truly told you this matter, and I humbly beseech you so to deal in it as the persuasions of nature, reason, wisdom, and Christianity shall inform you; and to accept the vows of one whom you may now raise or scatter—which are, that as my love is directed unchangeably upon her, so all my labours shall concur to her contentment, and to show my humble obedience to yourself.

"Yours in all duty and humbleness,

"J. DONNE.

"*From my lodging by the Savoy,*
2nd February 1601–2.

"*To the Right Worshipful* SIR GEORGE MORE, KT."

[The next letter, it will be observed, was written ten days later from the Fleet Prison, into which

Donne was thrown, immediately after the secret of the marriage was disclosed.]

II.

[JOHN DONNE *to the* Lord Keeper,
SIR THOMAS EGERTON.]

" To excuse my offence, or so much to resist the just punishment for it, as to move your lordship to withdraw it, I thought till now were to aggravate my fault. But since it hath pleased God to join with you in punishing thereof with increasing my sickness, and yet that He gives me now audience by prayer, it emboldeneth me also to address my humble request to your lordship, that you would admit into your favourable consideration how far my intentions were from doing dishonour to your lordship's house, and how unable I am to escape utter and present destruction, if your lordship judge only of effect and deed.

" My services never had so much worth in them as to deserve the favours wherewith they were paid; but they had always so much honesty as that only this hath stained them. Your justice hath been merciful in making me know my offence, and it hath much profited me that I am dejected, since then I am so entirely yours that even your disfavours have wrought good upon me. I humbly beseech you that all my good may proceed from your lordship, and that since Sir George More, whom I leave no humble way unsought to regain, refers all to your lordship, you would be pleased to lessen that correction which your just wisdom hath destined for me, and so to pity my

3

sickness and other misery as shall best agree with your honourable disposition.

" Almighty God accompany all your lordship's purposes, and bless you and yours with many good days.

" Your lordship's most dejected and poor servant,

"JOHN DONNE.

" FLEET, 12 *Febr.* 1601–2."

———

The following letter has only very recently come into my hands, and has never yet been printed. It shows that Donne at the date on which it was written quite expected that his offence would be condoned, and that his dismissal from the secretaryship would be revoked. Lord Ellesmere's refusal to reconsider the sentence he had passed evidently burst upon Donne as a thunderclap. On the 23rd of February he was evidently in high spirits, and believed that he would be reinstated in his office. Before a week had passed he quite realised that he was a ruined man.

This letter has been long in the possession of Miss Alicia Donne, of Chester. It bears the evidence of having been carelessly copied by some sixteenth-century scribe, who was not very familiar with Donne's hand. I copy it with all its errors, retaining the spelling. It was evidently addressed to Sir Henry Goodere of Polesworth :—

III.

" SIR,—Of myselfe (who, if honesty were precious, were worth the talking of) let me say a little. The Commissioners by Imprisoning the witnesses and excommunicating all us have implicitie [*sic*] instified our Marriage. Sir George will, as I heare, keepe her till

I send for her: and let her remayne there yett, his
good nature and her Sorrow will worke somethinge.
I have liberty to ride abrode and feele not much of
an Imprisonment. For my retorne to my L: and Sir
George his pacification, you know my meanes, and
therefore my hopes. Of Ostend, it is said there
hath been a new blow given . losses of men somwhat
equall, but the Enemy hath recovered a trench which
Sir Fr [Vere]: had held out of the Towne. The states
have honored him by publishing an Edict with sharpe
punishment to any that speke dishonorably of his
party with the Arch D: If the Emperor were dead
before you went, perchance he is buryed by this time.
I hope sombody els hath had the yll luck to tell you
first, that the yonge Bedford is dead. The K: of
Spaine intends to spend this Somer in Italy. And
there I thinke by that tyme wil be our Lords of Pembroke, Wylloughby, and Worster. The Lo: Deputy
hath cut off some of Tyrrels now lately but no greate
number. I send this Letter to aske the way to Polesworth: If I heare it finde it [*sic*], I shall cost you halfe
an houre a weeke to reade the rest. I heare nothing
of your Warrant from Mr. Andrew Lee. Take my love
and honesty into the good opinion, and comend my
poore unworthie thanks and service to your good Lady:
"23ᵈ *Febr:* 1601[-2]: from my chamber at Mr.
Haines his house by the Savoye (for this Language
your supscriptions use).
" Your true certeyne frind, Jo: Donne:"

Just a week after this letter was despatched, the
outlook had entirely changed. Hitherto Donne had

hardly realised the seriousness of the crisis, but the
Lord Keeper strongly resented the outrage done by
his secretary in entering into an engagement to
marry Sir George More's daughter whilst she was
actually an inmate at York House. Sir George was
prepared to make the best of the business. The
Lord Keeper would not condone it. He was inexorable, and Donne was dismissed with disgrace
from a position which he was eminently qualified
to fill, and was turned loose upon the world, to
begin life anew with a stain upon his name. The
following pathetic letter of remonstrance produced
no effect. It shows that the writer understood only
too well that his career was spoilt, and that he
had nothing to do but to submit to the inevitable
consequences of his serious misconduct.

IV.

· [Donne *to* Sir Thomas Egerton.]

"That offence, which was to God in this matter,
His mercy hath assured my conscience is pardoned.

"The Commissioners who minister His anger and
mercy incline also to remit it.[1]

"Sir George More, of whose learning and wisdom I
have good knowledge, and therefore good hope of his
moderation, hath said upon his last going that he was
so far from being any cause or mover of any punishment or disgrace, that if it fitted his reputation he
would be a suitor to your lordship for my restoring.

---

[1] The allusion is to the special Commissioners who were appointed
to report and adjudicate upon the validity of the marriage, and the
offence committed by the parties concerned.

All these irons are knocked off, yet I perish in as heavy fetters as ever whilst I languish under your lordship's anger.

"How soon my history is despatched! I was carefully and honestly bred; enjoyed an indifferent fortune; I had (and I had understanding enough to value it) the sweetness and security of a freedom and independency, without marking out to my hopes any place of profit. I had a desire to be your lordship's servant, by the favour which your good son's love to me obtained. I was four years your lordship's secretary, not dishonest nor greedy. The sickness of which I died is that I began in your lordship's house this love. When I shall be buried I know not. It is late now for me . . . to begin that course which some years past I purposed to travel,[1] though I could now do it not much disadvantageously. But I have some bridle upon me now more than then by my marriage of this gentlewoman; in providing for whom I can and will show myself very honest, though not so fortunate.

"To seek preferment here with any but your lordship were a madness. Every great man to whom I shall address any such suit will silently dispute the case, and say, 'Would any Lord Keeper so disgraciously have imprisoned him and flung him away if he had not done some other great fault of which we hear not?' So that to the burden of my true weaknesses I shall have this addition of a very prejudicial suspicion that I am worse than I hope your lordship doth think me, or would that the world should think. I have therefore no way before me, but must turn

---

[1] Referring to his earlier intention of adopting the profession of the law.

back to your lordship,—who knows that redemption was no less a work than creation.

"I know my fault so well, and so will acknowledge it, that I protest I have not so much as inwardly grudged or startled at the punishment. I know your lordship's disposition so well, as though in course of justice it be of proof against clamours of offenders, yet it is not strong enough to resist itself, and I know itself naturally inclines it to pity. I know mine own necessity, out of which I humbly beg your lordship will so much intender your heart towards me, as to give me leave to come into your presence. Affliction, misery, and destruction are not there; and everywhere else where I am they are.

"Your lordship's most poor and most penitent servant,

"J. DONNE.

"1 *Martii* 1601[-2].

"To the Right Honourable my very good Lord and Master, SIR THOMAS EGERTON, Knight, Lord Keeper of the Great Seal of England."

CHAPTER II

NOSCITUR A SOCIIS

DONNE AND HIS FRIENDS

WE have seen that the messenger who undertook to carry the news of Donne's marriage to Sir George More was the Earl of Northumberland, at that time one of the most conspicuous noblemen in England. The earl was a very munificent personage and a liberal patron of men of genius, especially such as shared his own enthusiasm for mathematical studies. Indeed, from his constant companionship with John Dee, the mathematician and visionary, and Thomas Harriott, the astronomer, the earl got to be known by the name of Harry the Wizard, and he was believed by the multitude to be a practiser of the black art. How this unfortunate nobleman became accused of complicity in the Gunpowder Plot, how he was cruelly plundered, heavily fined, and kept a prisoner for more than fifteen years in the Tower, while Sir Walter Raleigh was suffering from his long imprisonment in another part of the same grim fortress, and "taking exercise upon the leads," may be read in our ordinary handbooks of English history. During their long incarceration, these two illustrious victims of shameful oppression were allowed in each case to receive visitors

pretty freely, and the earl still managed to keep up
some little hospitality, and was surrounded by scholars
and men of bright intellect, who interested him in the
inquiries and discoveries that were going on outside.
That young John Donne was one of those who found
his way into the presence of his noble friend during
his captivity we cannot doubt.　At anyrate, some
months after his release from the Tower in 1621, we
find Donne dining with him at Sion House, where
Northumberland then resided.　It would be difficult
to believe that the friendly intercourse which had
been so close in 1600 would have been renewed after
twenty years, unless cordial relations had been kept
up between the two friends in the meantime.

In October 1600—less than a year after the death
of his second wife, who it will be remembered was Sir
George More's sister—the Lord Keeper took to himself
a third wife ; and this time the alliance was a splendid
one.　The lady whom he married was Alice, daughter
of Sir John Spencer of Althorpe, widow of Ferdinand,
fifth Earl of Derby, to whom she had borne three
daughters, co-heiresses to a great inheritance.　These
daughters became members of the Lord Keeper's
family, and took up their residence at York House.
The second, Frances, was promptly married to the
Lord Keeper's son, subsequently Earl of Bridgewater ;
the eldest, Ann, became the wife of Grey Brydges,
fifth Baron Chandos of Sudely, celebrated even in
that prodigal age for the profuseness of his hospitalities, and called the "King of the Cotswolds"; the third,
Elizabeth, three weeks after Donne's marriage, and
before the secret had been made known, became the
wife of Henry Hastings, fifth Earl of Huntingdon,

neither bride nor bridegroom having yet completed their
fifteenth year. It is significant that, so far from
Donne's relations with the Countess of Derby and her
daughters having become in any way weakened, or their
affection and admiration for him forfeited by his
marriage, they all continued among his devoted friends
to the end of their respective lives, Lady Huntingdon
especially being a frequent correspondent, and always
delighting in his society.

Lady Huntingdon grew to be one of the leaders of
fashion at the court of James I., and her salons were
frequented by men of letters and conversationalists,
who always found a cordial welcome.

There were many others among the nobility and
courtiers with whom Donne's duties as secretary to
the Lord Keeper brought him from time to time into
confidential intimacy. When Richard Herbert, Esq.,
of Montgomery Castle, died in 1596, leaving Edward
Herbert, afterwards Lord Herbert of Cherbury, as his
heir, Sir George More managed to procure for himself
the guardianship of the precocious lad, then a gentleman commoner at University College, Oxford, and in
his fifteenth year. In 1599 he married. A little
later his mother, Magdalen Herbert, took a house in
Oxford, and settled there with her large young family.
During this period Donne was apparently sent down
by the Lord Keeper on some matters of business,
probably connected with Sir George More's guardianship. It was Donne's first introduction to Mrs.
Herbert, and his first introduction, too, to her son,
George Herbert, who at this time was a boy of seven
or eight years old. The visit was the beginning of a
lifelong friendship with the Herberts—a friendship

which grew and strengthened and continued till the
end of Donne's life. He corresponded frequently
with Lord Herbert of Cherbury, bequeathed a ring
with one of the famous anchor seals to George Herbert,
then in residence at Bemerton; and in 1627 he
preached what may perhaps be called his most
pathetic and most eloquent sermon at the funeral of
Magdalen Herbert, who, by her second marriage, had
become Lady Danvers. It was probably through Sir
Edward Herbert that Donne became acquainted with
Sir Thomas Lucy, grandson of Shakespeare's Justice
Shallow, a gentleman of literary tastes and possessing
a large library. To him Donne addressed, as early as
1607, one of his most thoughtful and elaborate letters.

Donne's great patron and admirer at this earlier
period of his life, however, was Lucy, Countess of
Bedford, whom her contemporaries called "The
friend of the Muses." She was the daughter of Sir
John Harrington of Exton, the most considerable
magnate in the county of Rutland. Sir John claimed
descent from the Bruces, and the claim was allowed
by James I., who was never slow to receive into favour
those whom he considered to have royal blood in
their veins. His daughter Lucy was married in
1594 to Edward Russell, third Earl of Bedford; the
bride was in her teens, the bridegroom in his twentieth
year. He had succeeded to the earldom at the death
of his grandfather in 1585, and appears to have been
a man of no particular force of character; he was of
weakly constitution and retired habits, was paralysed
before he was thirty, and was quite content that his
countess should play her part in the gaieties of the
court, while he lived retired at Moor Park or Chenies.

The Countess of Bedford was one of the most lovely and gifted ladies of her time. Her ambition, above all things, was to be considered a patron of literature and literary men. The gardens at her house at Twickenham, where she kept up her hospitalities on a sumptuous scale, were famous for the assemblies of poets, wits, and whoever else happened to be the intellectual celebrities of the hour. She herself wrote verses—sometimes exchanging her own effusions with those of her guests who had presented her with a song or a sonnet. She exacted from her favourites the frequent homage of their offerings in letters and poems. She delighted in startling subjects of conversation, which others might take part in; her entertainments were veritable intellectual feasts, at which she presided as mistress of the board. Graceful and highly cultured, rich and lavish in her bounty, with a refined taste in art and literature, and always on the watch to attract men of genius to her side, it was not long before Donne found himself among the regular attendants at her court,—for at Twickenham the semblance of a court was kept up as if the Countess of Bedford had been a royal personage.

Lady Bedford appears to have taken up young Donne before his marriage,—how soon it is impossible to say. Her father's sister was the wife of Francis, Lord Hastings, and it was their son Henry, Earl of Huntingdon, who married Elizabeth, the Lord Keeper's stepdaughter and ward, of whom we have already spoken. Thus Lady Huntingdon and Lady Bedford were first cousins. This may perhaps have brought the young secretary under the personal notice of her ladyship; but so *fashionable* a man of letters as Donne had by this time become was not likely to escape the fascinations of the great lady, with her enthusiasm for literature, her eagerness to excel, her love of patronising notorieties, and her craving for admiration from those whose homage redounded to her glory. Donne soon became a constant guest at Twickenham, and, more than that, a dear friend and frequent correspondent of Lady Bedford. Unhappily, when the collection of Donne's letters was published by his worthless son in 1654, her ladyship had been dead more than twenty years; and her representatives were not likely to surrender to a profligate like the younger Donne the familiar and playful notes which had been addressed to the great lady in the gay and happy springtime of her married life. But as two of these early letters are good specimens of the epistolary style of the times,— so unlike our modern manner of expressing our sentiments, and so free from the slovenliness and careless hurry of our nineteenth-century correspondence,—I give them here as I find them. They were both written from Micham in 1607 or 1608.

To the COUNTESS OF BEDFORD.

" MADAM,—Amongst many other dignities which this letter hath by being received and seen by you, it is not the least, that it was prophesied of before it was born ; for your brother told you in his letter, that I had written: he did me much honour both in advancing my truth so far as to call a promise an act already done ; and to provide me a means of doing him a service in this act, which is but doing right to myself: for by this performance of mine own word I have also

justified that part of his letter which concerned me:
and it had been a double guiltiness in me to have made
him guilty towards you. It makes no difference that
this came not the same day, nor bears the same date
as his: for though in inheritances and worldly posses-
sions we consider the dates of evidences, yet in letters,
by which we deliver over our affections and assurances
of friendship, and the best faculties of our souls, times
and days cannot have interest nor be considerable,
because that which passes by them is eternal, and out
of the measure of time.

"Because therefore it is the office of this letter to
convey my best wishes and all the effects of a noble
love unto you (which are the best fruits that so poor
a soil, as my poor soul is, can produce), you may be
pleased to allow the letter thus much of the soul's
privilege, as to exempt it from straitness of hours, or
any measure of times, and so believe it came then.
And for my part, I shall make it so like my soul, that
as the affection of which it is the messenger, begun in
me without my knowing when, any more than I know
when my soul began: so it shall continue as long as that.

"Your most affectionate friend and servant,
"J. D."

To the same.

"HAPPIEST AND WORTHIEST LADY,—I do not remember
that ever I have seen a petition in verse; I would not
therefore be singular, nor add these to your other
papers. I have yet adventured so near as to make a
petition for verse, it is for those your ladyship did me
the honour [to show] me in Twickenham garden, except
you repent your making, and have mended your

judgment by thinking worse, that is, better, because juster of their subject. They must needs be an excellent exercise of your wit, which speak so well of so ill: I humbly beg them of your ladyship, with two such promises, as to any other of your compositions were threatenings: that I will not show them, and that I will not believe them: and nothing should be so used that comes from your brain or breast. If I should confesse a fault in the boldness of asking them, or make a fault by doing it in a longer letter, your ladyship might use your style and old fashion of the court towards me and pay with a pardon. Here, therefore, I humbly kiss your ladyship's fair learned hands, and wish you good wishes and speedy grants.

"Your ladyship's servant,

"J. Donne."

Donne continued to correspond with Lady Bedford for many years; some of his best poetry was addressed to her; she generously helped him with money more than once or twice when he needed it most. She stood as sponsor to one of his children, to whom she gave her own name.[1]   When Bridget, Lady Markham, her ladyship's cousin, died in May 1609, Donne wrote one of his best elegies upon the deceased; two months later he wrote no less than three poems on Miss Cecilia Bulstrode, one of the ladies-in-waiting to Queen Anne, who had fallen sick and died in Lady Bedford's house at an early age. It is probably that this was the occasion on which Lady Bedford was so affected by the poet's sympathy that she paid his debts in

[1] Lucy, Donne's second daughter, was baptized at Micham 8th August 1608.

acknowledgment of her gratitude. Some years later another sorrow came upon her. In August 1613 her father, Lord Harrington, died at Worms; and in the following February her brother, the second lord, died of the smallpox at Kew, leaving no heirs-male. Donne was evidently much moved by the loss his friend had sustained, and made use of the opportunity to write what he calls "Obsequies on the Lord Harrington." Of course the poem was meant for Lady Bedford's eye. It is addressed to her dead brother; and in view of the writer having by this time signified his intention of shortly taking holy orders, he closes with a kind of promise that he would write no more verse—

"Do not, fair soul, this sacrifice refuse,
   That in thy grave I do inter my muse;
   Which by my grief—great as thy worth—being cast
   Behind hand, yet hath spoke, and spoke her last."

Lady Bedford had first known Donne in his bright and joyous youth; he was a trifler then and a courtier, whom it was hard to look upon as anything more; she had not learned to see the real earnestness that lay below the surface, and could not at first, when she herself was beginning to feel sobered and saddened by her sorrow, bring herself to approve of her poet friend entering upon the ministry of Christ's Church: for a little, a very little while, something approaching to a cloud gathered over their friendship, but it soon passed off. Her ladyship learnt to see that in those early years she had not fathomed the depths of that noble nature: she lived to understand how worthy, and more than worthy, her friend was of all the confidence and affection she had bestowed upon him. The last occasion on which we hear of the two meeting was in May 1619. Lady Bedford was returning from Heidelberg, where she had been very seriously ill. Donne was himself on his way to Germany. Lady Bedford was at Antwerp, and she was lying in a darkened room suffering from some affection of the eyes. They parted—she to be met on her arrival in London by a great crowd, who turned out to welcome her on her recovery; he to present himself at the court of Elizabeth of Bohemia at Heidelberg, and to preach a memorable sermon, which has been preserved.

After this Lady Bedford lived comparatively a retired life at Moor Park in Hertfordshire, where her gardens became even more celebrated than those at Twickenham.

As late as 1622 Donne˜ was still corresponding with her. Her own letters from this time—and many have been preserved—exhibit an increasing seriousness of tone. She felt acutely the loss of relatives and friends, and latterly she suffered much from gout and other ailments.

But of all Donne's intimate associates who attached themselves to him in his years of struggle and disappointment, and who continued through life to feel the irresistible attractiveness of his sweet and affectionate nature,—the one man who found the way to his fullest confidence, the man from whom he had no secrets, and to whom he wrote with entire sympathy and without reserve, was Sir Henry Goodere of Polesworth in Warwickshire.

St. Edith's Abbey at Polesworth was a house of Benedictine nuns, which enjoyed an unusually good reputation when it was suppressed by the creatures of Henry VIII. in 1539. In the scramble that ensued, when the lands of the monasteries came into the market, the estates of this abbey were handed over to one Francis Goodere of London, Gent., who appears to have been a successful merchant in search of good investments. He acquired extensive estates in Warwickshire; but—as was so often observed in the case of the rich capitalists who bought up the lands of the monasteries—in the next generation there was only a single heir-male, upon whom all the property of his father and brother (the sons of the original Francis Goodere) was entailed on condition that he married his uncle's daughter, and so kept the estates *in the family*. This was our Sir Henry Goodere, who seems to have been knighted at the close of Queen Elizabeth's reign, and on the accession of James I. obtained the honorary appointment of a Gentleman of the Privy Chamber. He never rose to any higher position, though he was a courtier for many years, and joined in all the gaieties and extravagant amusements of the court, to the serious damage of his fortune, in so much that he appears to have died insolvent. Sir Henry was a gentleman of many accomplishments, with cultivated tastes, and of a poetic temperament; he had a large and apparently well-chosen library; but his almost romantic devotion to his friend has won for him an immortality which he could not otherwise have achieved. Donne's letters to him, numbering between forty and fifty, form the most precious portion of a correspondence which will always be regarded as a chapter in English literature we could ill spare, and which brings us into touch with the modes of thought, the subtile questionings, and the true sentiments and beliefs of a time

4

when England was in the transition period between the despotism of the Tudors and the social and political revolution that was coming.

As the collection of Donne's *Letters to Several Persons of Honour*, which were published in quarto in 1654, are not now easily procurable, I think it well to give here some few specimens of the letters to Sir Henry Goodere, which may serve as examples of the curiously stilted style in which correspondence was carried on three centuries ago, and at the same time furnish some insight into the inner life of one who for many years was face to face with difficulties of various kinds, such as weaker men would have sunk under, but which, in Donne's case, became, under God, only steps in the building up of his character. He bore his training bravely ; he learned his lessons wisely ; as he grew in depth of knowledge and breadth of view, " he gathered strength—at last he beat his music out."

It was not only among the nobility and the courtiers that Donne's irresistible attractiveness won him friends who stood by him, and were glad to enjoy his society. Among the great lawyers who were already in the first rank of the profession, or who were sure to attain eminence, Donne had early been recognised as a young man of supreme ability, and as likely to make a great reputation. Among these were Sir George Kingsmill, after whom, I conjecture, that Donne's second son George was named. He had married Lady Bedford's cousin, the mother of Henry, Earl of Huntingdon. Sir George, who was a Judge of the Court of Common Pleas, died in 1606,

but his lady continued on intimate terms with the
poet through life, and appears among his correspondents.
Sir Julius Cæsar has already been mentioned. He
became eventually Master of the Rolls; his extraordinary generosity is noticed by Weldon, and his
house at Micham was Donne's frequent resort. Others
of his familiars at this period were William Hakewill,
an extremely learned barrister, Solicitor-General to
Queen Anne of Denmark; Richard Martin, afterwards
Recorder of London ; and Sir William Jones, eventually
a Judge of the King's Bench, with many another whom
we may pass over.

But if the wits and the courtiers, the nobility, and
the luminaries of the law courts all agreed in their
high opinion of the young poet and courtier, there were
some, too, among the prominent divines and theologians who even thus early had begun to recognise
that this universal genius had the making in him of
a formidable controversialist, and whose counsel and
suggestions even in matters theological were worth
asking and worth attending to. Foremost among
these were Bishop Andrewes and Bishop Morton.

Andrewes was, at the time of Donne's marriage,
Rector of St. Giles's, Cripplegate, and a Prebendary of
St. Paul's ; he was already a frequent preacher in
London, and was noted for his ascetic life and
excessive devotion to study. Donne was his junior
by nearly twenty years, but this did not prevent the
elder man conceiving a cordial feeling of regard for
the younger ; and a friendship sprang up between them
which was honourable to both. Once, we learn,
Andrewes borrowed a book from Donne, which by
an accident fell into the hands of some children in the

house where he was staying. The urchins proceeded
to tear out some leaves of the volume, and, as a new
copy was not easily procurable, Andrewes wrote out
the torn pages with his own hand, and sent the book
back to its owner with the damaged portion replaced
in manuscript. The letter and Latin verses which
Donne sent to the future bishop acknowledging the
return of his book have survived ; but what would not
we give for that precious volume if we could handle it
ourselves ?

The intimacy with Bishop Morton must have begun
very soon after the death of Queen Elizabeth. Morton
was ten years Donne's senior, and, though now nearly
forty years of age, he had as yet published nothing.
Nevertheless, he had earned for himself a reputation
for learning and scholarship at Cambridge ; and when
he returned from a year's sojourn on the Continent, in
1603, he was well prepared to engage in the polemics
of the time, if any opportunity should arise. It was
not long in coming. The death of Queen Elizabeth
had given new hopes to the Ultramontane zealots in
England, and the Romanists began to give themselves
the airs of superiors who were entitled to instruct the
Anglican divines and let the world see how defenceless
the position of the Church of England was when
exposed to the attacks of the trained logicians of the
Jesuit colleges and the great luminaries of the new
theology.

It is not to be wondered at that the controversialists
on the other side of the channel should have made
the mistake of deeming that the Anglican theology
at this time had no champions qualified to stand
forth as its defenders. Since the death of Bishop

Jewel, in 1575, absolutely the only representative of theological learning in England who held any important Church preferment was Nowell, Dean of St. Paul's; he was now nearly one hundred years old, and had published his famous *Catechism* at the beginning of Queen Elizabeth's reign. Among the Puritan clergy there were many who were laborious preachers and diligent students of the Scriptures; but they and their Anglican opponents were wasting their strength in wrangling about the ceremonies and in curious questions regarding matters transcendental which profit not, for they are vain. One has only to run an eye down the pages of Le Neve, and note the names of those who were members of the cathedral chapters up and down the land, to understand the way in which ecclesiastical patronage was prostituted during the thirty years or so before the accession of James I. In the Cathedral Church of Canterbury during those thirty years not a single Englishman can be found among the deans, archdeacons, or prebendaries, who had the least claim to be considered a theologian. The one only member of the Chapter of Canterbury during the barren period who had any reputation for learning was Saravia, a foreigner, who held his stall from 1595 to 1602. At York, with its thirty-four prebendal stalls, there is not a man who can be pointed to of whom anything is known that is worth recording. Controversial theology in the Church of England seemed to be dead. To the outside world, to the English Jesuits, with Robert Parsons as their Coryphæus, it might well have seemed that all the intellect of the country was devoting itself to mere literary trifling. The time

had come once more to show the people that their
leaders were blind guides, by whom they had been led
astray. When James I. showed that he was by no
means inclined to throw himself into the arms of the
Roman faction, and when the detestable Gunpowder
Plot forced the Government to resort to strong
measures in self-defence, the Roman polemics began
their campaign through the printing-press; but the
gauntlet was no sooner thrown down than, no doubt
to the astonishment of those who had delivered their
attack, the challenge was taken up by a band of
scholars armed at all points, though their names had
hardly been heard of outside the limited circle in
which they had hitherto moved. Richard Hooker
was dead; he had published in 1597 his fifth book of
the immortal *Ecclesiastical Polity*, and dedicated it to
the Primate. What did Whitgift care for such as he ?
Hooker had been hunted out of the Mastership of the
Temple, and sent to rock the cradle and watch his
sheep at Bishopbourne, a short walk from Canterbury.
There Saravia seems to have been his only friend.
Some few bewailed him, and in their hearts cried
"Shame"; but they held their peace when it was
the time for silence. Donne read and absorbed
Hooker's great work, especially the first book,—
utilised it, made it his own, and reproduced it in his
Biathanatos,—but he never so much as mentioned
Hooker's name.

And yet there was a school of theology growing up
in the two universities, which was destined by and by
to send forth the glorious band of Anglican divines
who should prove themselves more than a match for
all the Roman gladiators. At Oxford there was

bitter dissension, almost before the queen had died, between Robert Abbot, afterwards Bishop of Salisbury, and Laud, then proctor of the university. The one a stubborn Calvinist, and exceedingly learned ; the other the intrepid Reformer, who claimed that the Church of England should in ritual and discipline be brought back to what she had been in her better days : so only could she hope to deal with the sophistries and corruptions of Rome. At Cambridge the influence of Perkins, the able and earnest Calvinist, had been an immeasurable force in awakening spiritual life in the university ; but it was Andrewes to whom the divinity students came in crowds to take down his catechetical lectures at Pembroke, of which he was tutor. Meanwhile, at St. John's College the study of divinity was being pursued by the great majority of Fellows with so much eagerness that the college had almost become a theological seminary. When James I. came to the throne three of the bishops were St. John's men ; and during the next twenty years no less than eight more Johnians were raised to the Episcopate. They were the very best appointments the king made during his reign ; they were all men of conspicuous learning and high character, such as the Church of England had not known for many a long day. Of these eight Dr. Morton was one, though he had to wait some years for his promotion. The revival of interest in theology, and the hitherto unheard-of care and discretion in exercising church patronage, soon brought the ablest men to the front ; and the stimulus given to the study of divinity, which Donne alludes to in one of his *Problems*, made theology fashionable among all classes.

Men dragged their religion into all they talked and
all they wrote about, it gave a tinge to all their
lighter utterances in prose or verse.   If this was not
all gain, at anyrate it was not all loss.

The necessity of taking strong measures against
the *Popish Recusants*, as they were called, who refused
on conscientious grounds to take the new oath of
allegiance, brought out a number of protests more or
less offensive from the Roman party.   It was judged
necessary to meet these books and pamphlets with
prompt rejoinders.   Dr. Morton threw himself into
the fray with a vigour and readiness which made his
services peculiarly valuable.   It is impossible here to
enter into the literary history of the controversies of
the time.   In three years, at least six books, or pamphlets, some in English, some in Latin, appeared,
having Dr. Morton's name on the title, all overflowing
with learning, and all dealing heavy blows at Parsons
and his friends.   They never could have been written
by one man single-handed.   It was notorious that
the Roman disputants helped one another in their
attacks.   It was plain that there must be co-operation
among the Anglicans to foil their assailants.   Morton
found in Donne a most able and willing coadjutor.
For years the younger man had been sedulously and
thoughtfully studying the points in dispute between
the Church of England and the Papacy; he had been
buying books largely and reading them closely,
annotating and abstracting, as Walton expresses it;
"cribrating and re-cribrating and post-cribrating," as
he himself says.   All this accumulation of learned
lore, written in the small and beautiful hand which
never varies, and with all the references minutely set

down on the margin of his manuscripts, where a blot
or a correction is a thing unknown, was accessible
and ready for use at any moment. Even if we had
not been told that he gave Morton constant and
valuable help, a comparison of the authorities quoted
and referred to in Morton's *Catholic Appeal*, with those
set down in Donne's *Pseudo Martyr*, would have
convinced a careful reader of the fact. The curious
and out-of-the-way books cited in both works are
very numerous, and not to be found elsewhere.

As the two worked on, the king with his very
considerable theological training—pedantry you may
call it if you will—could not but be interested in
their task. James formed a strong opinion that this
gifted young scholar had a vocation, but his view of
what that vocation was was not Donne's view. It
seems that the king had expressed his opinion very
early, that the young courtier must stick to divinity
and give up his ambition to rise in the diplomatic
service. In June 1607 Morton got his first preferment; he was offered, and accepted, the Deanery of
Gloucester. Nine years before this, George, Earl of
Huntingdon, had procured for him the living of Long
Marston in Yorkshire, a benefice of some value.
Morton immediately sent for his friend, and then and
there offered to resign the living if Donne could but
bring himself to take holy orders, as he advised him
in all seriousness and affection to do. The interview
is beautifully described by Walton; but what Morton
advised was not yet to be. At the end of three days,
which had been given him to consider the proposal,
Donne gratefully but firmly declined; his conscience
he would not tamper with; and to enter the ministry

of Christ's Church only for the hope of gain,—that he could not, and would not, bring himself to do. It might be the call of man, it was not the call of God. So Morton went to his deanery, and Donne went back to the little home at Micham, and continued his attendance at the court, resisting and rebelling against that gracious leading of God's providence, which in the end bore him along the road that he was so eminently fitted to travel.

CHAPTER III

STEPS TO THE ALTAR

DONNE ceased to reside with Sir Francis Wooley some time in 1605. There were more reasons than one for this removal. Not only was the distance from London a serious inconvenience to a young courtier on the look-out for preferment, but Donne's family was increasing upon him; two children had already been born, and a third was on the way. In February 1605 he received an invitation to travel abroad with three gentlemen of large means, who were starting on a Continental tour, and who needed some one to act as their interpreter and give them the benefit of his experience. The party held a licence for a three-years' absence, and took servants and horse with them. Unfortunately, we know nothing more about this journey; but we do know that, whatever happened to his companions, Donne was at home again in 1606, and, with his wife and children, living at Micham. The house in which he continued to reside for the next three or four years was still standing in 1840, and was then known as " Donne's House." It belonged then to the Simpson family, and it was pulled down some few years later. The illustration on the opposite page is a reproduction of a sketch by my lamented friend, the late

Mr. Richard Simpson, author of the *Life of Edmund Campion*, who as a boy often played in the garden, and who was taught to believe that some of the trees then standing had been planted during Donne's tenancy.

On his return from this short absence he found himself without any employment, and his comparatively small income compelled him to look about for some means of adding to his resources. His friends came round him, and did for him what they could; and, according to the fashion of the time, he set himself to seek for new patrons by placing his pen at the disposal of those whose vanity or ambition called for such literary assistance as he could give. Meanwhile, he was pursuing his reading with ceaseless industry. There had been a time when he had devoted himself very earnestly to the study of the law, for he had originally intended to adopt the legal profession; but during his four years as secretary to the Lord Keeper his thoughts and pursuits had necessarily been turned in another direction; and he now threw himself more than ever before into historic theology and casuistry. His early training, under the eye of his Jesuit uncle, had doubtless cultivated and stimulated the natural subtlety of his intellect. He could never be satisfied with a superficial treatment of any subject, or take his opinions upon trust without patient scrutiny. He was one of those men who always find it hard to "run in harness"; a man of original genius; in fact, who must needs take his own course in dealing with any question that presented itself, and who found himself always going to the root of things, and was almost morbidly restless and ill-at-ease till he had discovered some solution of his own for such difficulties as perplexed him. It was irksome and distasteful to him to follow the beaten track and tread in the footsteps of others, leaving himself simply to follow where they led.

It is significant that during these Micham days we still find him occasionally distributing those *Problems* of which — perhaps fortunately — only a few have survived. They have, indeed, a certain interest for us, in that they reflect the working of the writer's mind at this time. They show him to us, not so much inclined to scepticism as feeling his way towards some positive basis of truth. Seeking for certainties and finding none, he is in the stage when any *system* of philosophy does not satisfy the intellect—the stage when an inquirer tends to become a mere eclectic, always inquiring, always seeing objections, always surprising others with unexpected doubts and difficulties, always prone to provoke and irritate shallow minds with what seem to them mere intellectual quibbles and paradoxes.

In one of his letters he mentions that he had been engaged upon a small collection of *Cases of Conscience* —exercises, that is, in casuistry; a branch of ethical theology to which our English divines have so seldom given their attention, and which, indeed, since Jeremy Taylor wrote his *Ductor Dubitantium*, none of them have busied themselves with, though that, too, may come up again some day. These "cases" have never seen the light, and are not likely to be recovered now.

During these Micham days there is a tone of mournfulness in his letters, attributable far less to any mere lack of means than to that intellectual depression inseparable from excessive strain upon the powers of brain and heart. He read late into the night; he wrote sometimes "in the noise of three gamesome children," with his wife by his side. He speaks of his "thin little house," as if there could be no quiet in it; but he had a very large collection of books, and he found no difficulty in borrowing largely from others.

Of course there would come, under such circumstances, to the student, overwrought and never enjoying robust health, moods of depression, weariness, despondency; and at the worst, the old thought would intrude itself upon him: "Were it not better not to be?"

That the temptation to put an end to his own life ever presented itself to Donne in the form of a possible course of action—much less as a deliberate purpose to which his will inclined — must always appear incredible to any who have learned to know the man, and to appreciate the true nobility of his character. Yet, as a question for casuists, it still remained to be discussed as it never had been even by the most adventurous of the schoolmen, whether suicide, under no conceivable circumstances, could become excusable or cease to be accounted *in foro conscientiæ*, an unpardonable sin and crime.

Donne set himself to deal with this the greatest and most hazardous of all *cases of conscience*. The very novelty of the subject was doubtless to him its chief fascination. He attacked it from the point of view of an idealist, and an idealist only. When he had brought the inquiry to a close it had grown into a volume, bristling with references to an immense

number of authors whose works he had consulted—
not only consulted, but read, and weighed, and
pondered. He called the book, *Biathanatos: A
Declaration of that Paradox or Thesis, that Self-
homicide is not so naturally sin that it may never be
otherwise.* The work was written between 1606 √
and 1608, and for some years was kept under lock
and key, and appears to have been shown to very few
even of his closest friends. It was not till his
setting out to Germany in 1619 that he sent one
copy, in his own handwriting, to Sir Edward Herbert
(afterwards Lord Herbert of Cherbury),[1] and another
to Sir Robert Carr, afterwards Earl of Ancrum. A
third copy fell into the hands of his eldest son, John,
who, disregarding his father's wishes, and with characteristic brutality, made merchandise of it, and caused
it to be published in 4to in 1644.

Donne sent the manuscript of the *Biathanatos* to
Sir Robert Carr, with the following letter :—

" . . . Besides the poems, of which you took a
promise, I send you another book, to which there belongs this history : it was written by me many years
since; and because it is upon a misinterpretable subject,
I have always gone so near suppressing it as that it is
only not burnt. No hand hath passed upon it to copy
it, nor many eyes to read it; only to some particular
friends in both universities then when I writ it I
did communicate it; and I remember I had their
answer, that certainly there was a false thread in it,
but not easily found. Keep it, I pray, with the same
jealousy. Let any that your discretion admits to the

---

[1] Lord Herbert, in 1642, presented this copy to the Bodleian Library,
where it still remains.

sight of it know the date of it, and that it is a book written by *Jack Donne*, and not by *Dr. Donne*. Preserve it for me if I live, and if I die I only forbid it the press and the fire. Publish it not, but yet burn it not; and between those do what you will with it."

The *Biathanatos* is the most carefully constructed and closely reasoned of all Donne's writings, and · exhibits an extraordinary width and variety of curious learning. That it. should ever be an attractive book is hardly to be expected; on the other hand, the thesis is so cautiously handled and so delicately, that the reading of the book could hurt no one. It is a literary curiosity—a *tour de force* unique in English literature, a survival of the old dialectic disputations, carried on strictly according to the rules of syllogistic reason, which the mediæval schoolmen loved so well.

Just about the time that this book was written, Donne was brought into that close intimacy with Dr. Morton which led to the offer being made him of the living of Long Marston. It is difficult to believe that Morton's proposal to resign this benefice, on his receiving the Deanery of Gloucester, could have been made without the cognisance of the king. I incline to think, indeed, that it was made at His Majesty's suggestion. As we have seen, it was gratefully declined.

If we may trust to Walton for the date of this incident, it was not many days after its occurrence that Donne was exerting himself to obtain an appointment, *not* in the king's household, but in that of Queen Anne of Denmark. The queen's secretary was a certain William Fowler, whose only qualification for

the office which he held was that he was a good
linguist. A knowledge of European languages was
essential for the management of the queen's correspondence. Mr. Fowler had received his appointment
immediately on the king's coming into England, and
had now held it for four years. From what we know
of the man, he can hardly have had an agreeable berth
in the household, for he was a fantastic coxcomb, and
a likely person to be the object of a good deal of
ridicule. Fowler, however, had no serious thought of
resigning without making terms with his successor;
and he appears to have made an extravagant demand
as a condition of his vacating his post. The negotia-
tion fell through.

During the next year or two, Donne made many other
unsuccessful attempts to get employment under the
crown. At one time he hoped to obtain the post of Secretary for Ireland; at another he had some hope of being
sent on an embassy to Venice or the Low Countries;
once he even thought of applying for an appointment
in the colony of Virginia. It was all in vain; one, and
only one, road to advancement was open to him. The
king turned a deaf ear to all the solicitations of his
friends. If not Church preferment, then none at all.

As the years went by, and the controversies between
the faction of the Roman recusants, who stubbornly
refused to take the Oath of Allegiance on the one side,
and the supporters of royal supremacy in Church and
State on the other, were become more and more acri-
monious; while, too, everybody—learned and simple
—was talking theology, and the perpetual sermons of
the court preachers were being attended by the king

5

and the nobility, and being discussed and criticised
without reserve; and while everybody was asking
when the new translation of the Bible would. be
finished, and what changes would be introduced,
Donne must have gradually got to see that it could
only be a question of time when he would be obliged
to give way; his scruples must have been slowly
getting overborne by the remorseless logic of facts.

As early as 1607 he had expressed very frankly to
a friend—probably Sir Henry Goodere, who himself, as
it seems, was troubled by some doubts and perplexities
of his own—what his religious position was:—

"You know I never fettered nor imprisoned the
word religion; not straightening it friarly, *Ad religiones factitias* (as the Romans call well their orders of
religion), not immuring it in a Rome, or a Wittenberg,
or a Geneva; they are all virtual beams of one sun,
and wheresoever they find clay hearts, they harden
them, and moulder them into dust; and they entender
and mollify waxen. They are not so contrary as the
north and south poles; and that they are connatural
pieces of one circle. Religion is Christianity, which
being too spiritual to be seen by us, doth therefore
take an apparent body of good life and works, so
salvation requires an honest Christian. These are the
two elements, and he which is elemented from these
hath the complexion of a good man, and a fit friend.
The diseases are, too much intention into indiscreet
zeal, and too much remissness and negligence by giving
scandal: for our condition and state in this, is as
infirm as in our bodies; where physicians consider
only two degrees; sickness, and neutrality; for there

is no health in us. This, sir, I used to say to you, rather to have so good a witness and corrector of my meditations, than to advise; and yet to do that too, since it is pardonable in a friend: not to slack you towards those friends which are religious in other clothes than we (for *amici vitia si feras facis tua*, is true of such faults); but to keep you awake against such as the place where you must live will often obtrude, which are not only naked, without any fashion of such garments, but have neither the body of religion, which is moral honesty and sociable faithfulness, nor the soul, Christianity. I know not how this paper escaped last week, which I send now; I was so sure that I enwrapped it then, that I should be so still, but that I had but one copy; forgive it as you used to do. From Micham in as much haste, and with as ill pen and ink, as the letter can excuse me of; but with the last and the next week's heart and affection.—Yours, very truly and affectionately,

" J. DONNE."

This is the language of one whose leanings were all towards a large and fearless toleration, but for such toleration the times were not ready; the writer was clearly a man before his age.

Meanwhile, the aggressive tone of the English Jesuits, and their fierce attacks upon the king and his policy, made it increasingly difficult for the Anglican divines to maintain a pacific attitude. Robert Parsons was forcing the hands of his own party and of the loyalists at the same moment. The provocation became ever greater and greater, and a feeling of bitter hostility was growing up, not against the con-

scientious refusers of the Oath of Allegiance, which
James I. in sheer self-defence had been compelled to
enforce, but against the Jesuit wing of the great
Ultramontane. army, whose champions disdained to
accept mere toleration, and would hear of nothing
short of supremacy.

Half angrily, half contemptuously, Donne at this
time wrote off his rather fierce little diatribe, entitled
" Ignatius his Conclave or his Inthronisation in a late
Election in Hell; wherein many things are mingled
by way of satire, concerning—(1) the Disposition of
Jesuits; (2) the Creation of a New Hell; (3) the
Establishing of a Church in the Moon." The tractate
was a *jeu d'esprit*, not in very good taste, and modelled
upon Seneca's *Ludus de Morte Claudii*, and was originally written in Latin, though an English version was
made for the unlearned, and printed at the same time.
The date of composition can hardly be later than
1608. More than one issue of it appeared from time
to time, and there is reason to suspect that the
earliest editions were pirated. Though the bookling
has little merit, it possesses a certain interest as an
indication of the way in which Donne's feeling against
the Romanists became gradually stronger, and his
position as an Anglican getting more and more clearly
defined and intelligible as the years ran on.

The sequence of events in Donne's life between
1606 and 1610 is difficult to make out with any
certainty; but we know that he was on intimate
terms with Sir Francis Bacon during this period, and
apparently employed by that illustrious man to
revise some of his books before they received their
final corrections. It was through Bacon, too, as he

tells us in one of his letters, that Donne was first introduced to James Hay, afterwards Earl of Carlisle. Lord Hay was for some years the reigning favourite at the court of King James, and he soon conceived a strong regard, which eventually developed into an affectionate friendship, for Donne. Hay, we learn, "took him into his service;" by which we are to understand that he became the great man's private secretary, with an assured income, and the duty of attending his patron at court. Hay was at this time *Master of the Wardrobe*, and this office necessitated his being frequently in the royal presence; and where he went, there his secretary was in attendance upon his patron. So it came about that Donne would be called upon to take his part in those *symposia*, of which Bishop Hacket gives us the following curious account:—

"His Majesty's table for the most part at times of repast was (as Constantine's court, *ecclesiæ instar*) a little university compassed with learned men of all professions, and His Majesty in the midst of them . . . *a living library*, furnished at all hands to reply, answer, object, resolve, discourse, explain, according to several occasions, emergent upon fact, or accidental upon speech."

In other words, the discussions during meals were kept up with interest and animation; and when an opinion was asked it had to be given on the spur of the moment. The scholars and divines in waiting were liable at any moment to be subject to a severe *viva voce* examination, were called upon to give chapter and verse for all they asserted, and to produce on the instant all they knew. It was in consequence of a

remark thrown out at one of these discussions that
Donne received a command from the king to set
down in writing the suggestions and arguments which
he had brought forward on the never-ending question
of the Oath of Allegiance. His way of putting the
case had struck James I. as especially original and
likely to prove effective against the Roman controversialists.

Walton assures us that in six weeks the royal
commands had been obeyed; and in the spring of
1610 *The Pseudo Martyr* appeared, a quarto volume
of nearly four hundred pages. The work was almost
immediately recognised as the most solid and masterly
contribution to the literature of a discussion which
had already been taken part in by the ablest and
most famous divines of the Church of England.

The view which Donne had set himself to support
was :—" That no pretence of conversion at first ;
assistance in the conquest ; or acceptation of any
surrender from any of our kings,—can give the pope
any more right over the kingdom of England, than
over any other free state whatsoever." Further,
that the punishments incurred by those who refuse to
obey the laws of the realm, and the sufferings they
bring upon themselves by their disobedience to those
laws under whose protection they live, *can never*
entitle them to be called martyrs ; for " the refusal of
the Oath of Allegiance doth corrupt and vitiate the
integrity of the whole act, and despoils them of the
interest and title to martyrdom."

The controversy, with all its subtleties, has long
ceased to have any but a historic interest ; but even
in our own days it is impossible to read Donne's

Advertisement to the Reader and the introductory preface without being profoundly touched by the allusions to the author's early difficulties on the one hand, and by the solemn tone of sad expostulation with those against whom he is writing on the other. Throughout the whole volume there is a self-restraint and dignity in carrying on the argument which are in marked contrast to the methods of discussion almost universally prevalent among the disputants on the one side or the other who had hitherto taken part in the controversies of the day.

At the close of the preface, Donne breaks forth into the following earnest and beautiful appeal to those with whom he had been arguing.

"I call to witness against you those whose testimony God Himself hath accepted.—Speak then and testify—O you glorious and triumphant army of martyrs, who enjoy now a permanent triumph in heaven, which knew the voice of your Shepherd, and stayed till He called, and went then with all alacrity: Is then any man received into your blessed legion by title of such a death as sedition, scandal, or any human respect occasioned? Oh no! For they which are in possession of that crown are such as have washed their garments, not in their own blood only (for so they might still remain red and stained), but in the blood of the Lamb which changes them to white. . . . That which Christian religion hath added to old philosophy—which was *to do no wrong*—is in this point no more than this, to keep our mind in an habitual preparation *to suffer wrong*, but not to urge and provoke and importune affliction so much as to make those punishments just, which otherwise had been wrongfully inflicted upon us. We are not sent into this world *to suffer* but *to do*, and to perform the offices of society required by our several callings. . . . Thus much I was willing to premit, to awaken you, if it please you to hear it, to a just love of your own safety, of the peace of your country, of the honour and reputation of your countrymen, and of the integrity of that which you call the Catholic cause and to acquaint you so far with my disposition and temper as that you need not be afraid to read my poor writings, who join you with mine own soul in my prayers, that your obedience here may prepare your admission into the heavenly Jerusalem, and that by the same obedience, *your days may be long in the land which the Lord your God hath given you.*"

The *Pseudo Martyr* was received with profound appreciation by the Anglican theologians of the time: scholars and men of learning could not but admire the originality of the writer, who had struck out a new line of argument and taken up a position from which he could not be dislodged. The Jesuits abroad at one time had intended to answer the book; but the truth is, it was unanswerable, and to pass it by in silence or with a depreciating sneer was deemed the safer course. The University of Oxford, however, in recognition of the author's conspicuous ability and learning, by decree of convocation conferred upon him the honorary degree of M.A. [18th April 1610]; the words of the grace setting forth that " it was for the credit of the university that such men as he who had deserved so well of the Church and State should be distinguished by academic honours."

When the *Pseudo Martyr* was presented in its

completeness to the king, once again he pressed upon
Donne his advice that he should take holy orders. This
time there could be no mistaking the significance of
the counsel given—it almost amounted to a royal
command. Even so he could not bring himself to
obey. He was haunted by morbid scruples; he could
not trust himself; he shrank from the thought that men
would attribute to him base and unworthy motives.

He had formed so high an ideal of the standard
which the "priest to the temple," as George Herbert
styled it, should attain to, that he could not bring
himself to embrace a life to which as yet he felt
no inner call. What form his answer to the king
took we shall never know; but that he excused
himself on the ground of his unfitness for the
ministry is certain. For the present there was an end
of the matter.

Another year passed away. Lord Hay, with the
shrewdness that characterised him, had become
convinced that he could do nothing for his friend as
long as he obstinately refused to enter upon the
only career which the king had marked out for him,
and the less so when it was evident that a new
favourite was now all-powerful at court and his own
personal influence was on the wane. Robert Carr—a
kinsman of Donne's friend of the same name, who
became Earl of Ancrum in 1633 — was created
Viscount Rochester on the 25th March 1611, being
the first Scotchman promoted to a seat in the English
House of Lords. He was now the most influential
personage with the king—not excepting even Lord
Salisbury, whose health was declining. Lord Hay saw
plainly that if Donne could commend himself to

the king's bosom friend there might still be a
chance of promotion somewhere.   But how to proceed
was the question.   Two letters in Tobie Matthew's
collection give us a clue to what happened.   It looks
as if the king was displeased with Donne for his
refusal to follow the advice tendered so emphatically.
To surrender at last would be flattering to James, but
to make Rochester the channel of communicating to
the king his submission would be a piece of delicate
flattery to the favourite.   Accordingly, some time
during the summer of 1611, Donne addressed a letter
to the great man, enclosing it in another to Lord Hay.
The tenor of both letters is the same—that to Lord
Rochester begins as follows:—

" MY LORD,—I may justly fear that your lordship
hath never heard of the name which lies at the
bottom of this letter, nor could I come to the boldness
of presenting it now without another boldness of
putting his lordship who now delivers it to that office.
Yet I have (or flatter myself to have) just excuses of
this and just ground of that ambition.   For having
obeyed at last, after much debatement within me, the
inspiration (as I hope) of the spirit of God, and
resolved to make my profession divinity, I make
account that I do but tell your lordship what God
hath told me, which is, that it is in this course, if in
any, that my service may be of use to this Church
and State.

" Since, then, your lordship's virtues have made you
so near the head in the one and so religious a member
of the other, I came to this courage of thrusting
myself thus into your lordship's presence, both in

respect that I was an independent and disobliged man towards any other person in this State, and delivered over now (in my resolution) to be a household servant of God."

It is obvious that this letter was meant to be laid before the king as an intimation that the writer had at last made up his mind to be ordained. Nevertheless, I find it impossible to resist the conviction that Rochester, so far from encouraging Donne to carry out his purpose, actually suppressed the letter, took him at once into his service, treated him with great liberality, and held out distinct hopes that he would yet be able to procure for him some valuable post at court. In other letters to the same nobleman, Donne, during the next year or so, again and again speaks of the obligations which he was under to his new patron, reminding him that *he had inspired new hopes* into him, telling him that there was this or that post likely to be vacant, which he desired to obtain, and excusing himself for asking for it on the ground that Rochester had encouraged him to apply for such preferment as he might desire to obtain. Rochester had evidently counted upon his influence with the king to save Donne from taking orders at all. But the king had made up his mind, and not even the favourite could induce him to change it. Meanwhile, Donne was unsettled, anxious, and the eternal want of pence was harassing him. Hope deferred was making his heart sick.

Just about this time another circumstance occurred which helped to turn him from the purpose he had formed of dedicating himself to the ministry of the Church.

At the close of the year 1610 the only child of Sir Robert Drury of Hawsted in Suffolk, one of the richest men in England, had died, in her sixteenth year, to the deep sorrow of her parents, who appeared inconsolable at their loss. Up to this time Donne had known little or nothing of Sir Robert, and had never seen the young lady; but, touched by the grief of the parents, and probably at the suggestion of some friend, he set himself to write an elegy upon the departed. She had been dead a year when the poem was presented to Sir Robert; and it was apparently printed at his expense. It was entitled "The First Anniversary: An Anatomy of the World, wherein, by occasion of the Untimely Death of Mistress Elizabeth Drury, the Frailty and the Decay of this whole World is represented." The poem is written in a style of extravagant panegyric, but it evidently gave unqualified pleasure to those for whom it was intended. No doubt Donne was handsomely rewarded for his work; but when, a little later, he offered to Sir Robert (who was a very vain man, and very greedy for notoriety) "The Second Anniversary," there was no bounds to his gratitude. Nothing was too much for him to do to reward the court poet for his services. "The First Anniversary" appears to have attracted not much notice. It was otherwise with the second, which appears to have been received with some adverse criticism. In a letter to Sir Henry Goodere, Donne thus replies to some of their strictures :—

"I doubt not but they will soon give over that part of that indictment which is that I have said so much; for nobody can imagine that I, who never saw her, could have any other purpose in that, than that, when I had received so very good testimony of her worthiness, and was gone down to print verses, it became me to say, not what I was sure was just truth, but the best that I could conceive; for that had been a new weakness in me to have praised anybody in printed verses that had not been capable of the best praise that I could give."

Meanwhile, Sir Robert Drury, hearing that the poet's family had by this time outgrown the accommodation of the little Micham house, and that he was too straitened in his means to take a larger one, generously offered to give Donne, with his wife and children, an asylum in Drury House, a magnificent mansion, lying just outside the city, and to the north-west of Temple Bar. There, for the next three or four years, he continued to reside as his home. I suspect the change unsettled him; that at Drury House he was less his own master than he had been heretofore, and that quiet retirement was difficult and often impossible. In point of fact, one of the first claims that his new friend made upon him was that he should accompany himself and Lady Drury on a foreign tour, on which the party set out in December 1611. It was then that Donne wrote the exquisite stanzas which he entitled " The Valediction," perhaps the best known of all his poems.

"A VALEDICTION, FORBIDDING TO MOURN.

"As virtuous men pass mildly away,
And whisper to their souls to go,
Whilst some of their sad friends do say,
'Now his breath goes,' and some say, 'No,'

"So let us melt, and make no noise,
    No tear-floods nor sigh-tempests move.
'Twere profanation of our joys
    To tell the laity our love.

"Moving of th' earth brings harms and fears,
    Men reckon what it did and meant;
But trepidations of the spheres,
    Tho' greater far, are innocent.

"Dull sublunary lovers' love—
    Whose soul is sense—cannot admit
Absence, because that doth remove
    Those things which elemented it.

"But we, by a love so far refined,
    That ourselves know not what it is,
Inter-assured of the mind,
    Care less hands, eyes, or lips to miss.

"Our two souls, therefore, which are one,—
    Though I must go,—endure not yet
A breach, but an expansion,
    Like gold to airy thinness beat.

"If we be two,—we are two—so
    As stiff twin compasses are two,
Thy soul, the fix'd foot, makes no show
    To move, but does, if the other do.

"And though thine in the centre sit,
    Yet, when my other far does roam,
Thine leans and hearkens after it,
    And grows erect as mine comes home.

"Such wilt thou be to me, who must,
    Like th' other foot, obliquely run:
Thy firmness makes my circle just,
    And makes me end where I begun."

The travellers crossed the Channel to Dieppe, passed
through Amiens, and thence to Paris, where Donne

fell seriously ill; and it seems that at this time the incident occurred which Isaak Walton has so graphically described, and which can only be read in his own words :—

" At this time of Mr. Donne's and his wife's living in Sir Robert's house, the Lord Hay was, by King James, sent upon a glorious embassy to the then French king, Henry the Fourth; and Sir Robert put on a sudden resolution to accompany him to the French court, and to be present at his audience there. And Sir Robert put on a sudden resolution to solicit Mr. Donne to be his companion in that journey. And this desire was suddenly made known to his wife, who was then with child, and otherwise under so dangerous a habit of body as to her health, that she professed an unwillingness to allow him any absence from her, saying, ' Her divining soul boded her some ill in his absence,' and therefore desired him not to leave her. This made Mr. Donne lay aside all thoughts of the journey, and really to resolve against it. But Sir Robert became restless in his persuasions for it, and Mr. Donne was so generous as to think he had sold his liberty when he received so many charitable kindnesses from him, and told his wife so ; who did therefore, with an unwilling willingness, give a faint consent to the journey, which was proposed to be but for two months; for about that time they determined their return. Within a few days after this resolve, the ambassador, Sir Robert, and Mr. Donne, left London, and were the twelfth day got all safe to Paris. Two days after their arrival there, Mr. Donne was left alone in that room in which Sir Robert and he and some other friends had dined to-

gether. To this place Sir Robert returned within
half an hour; and as he left, so he found, Mr. Donne
alone, but in such an ecstasy, and so altered as to his
looks, as amazed Sir Robert to behold him; insomuch
that he earnestly desired Mr. Donne to declare what
had befallen him in the short time of his absence.
To which Mr. Donne was not able to make a present
answer; but, after a long and perplexed pause, did at
last say: 'I have seen a dreadful vision since I saw
you; I have seen my dear wife pass twice by me
through this room, with her hair hanging about her
shoulders, and a dead child in her arms: this I have
seen since I saw you.' To which Sir Robert replied,
'Sure, sir, you have slept since I saw you; and this
is the result of some melancholy dream, which I desire
you to forget, for you are now awake.' To which Mr.
Donne's reply was: 'I cannot be surer that I now
live than that I have not slept since I saw you; and
am as sure that at her second appearing she stopped
and looked me in the face and vanished.' Rest and
sleep had not altered Mr. Donne's opinion the next
day; for he then affirmed this vision with a more
deliberate and so confirmed a confidence that he inclined Sir Robert to a faint belief that the vision was
true. It is truly said that desire and doubt have no
rest, and it proved so with Sir Robert; for he immediately sent a servant to Drury House, with a
charge to hasten back and bring him word whether
Mrs. Donne were alive, and, if alive, in what condition
she was as to her health. The twelfth day the
messenger returned with this account: that he found
and left Mrs. Donne very sad and sick in her bed;
and that, after a long and dangerous labour, she had

been delivered of a dead child. And, upon examination, the abortion proved to be the same day and about the very hour that Mr. Donne affirmed he saw her pass by him in his chamber.

"This is a relation that will beget some wonder, and it well may; for most of our world are at present possessed with an opinion that visions and miracles are ceased. And, though it is most certain that two lutes, being both strung and tuned to an equal pitch, and then one played upon, the other that is not touched being laid upon a table at a fit distance, will, like an echo to a trumpet, warble a faint audible harmony in answer to the same tune, yet many will not believe there is any such thing as a sympathy of souls; and I am well pleased that every reader do enjoy his own opinion."

The foreign tour came to an end in August 1612, and Donne, on his return to England, found Lord Rochester in greater favour with the king than ever. Lord Salisbury had died on the 24th May, and Rochester had virtually succeeded him to his post as secretary. The great addition to the work thus thrown upon the new minister (as we may venture to call him) made him perhaps more difficult of approach; for, shortly after his return from abroad, Donne found it necessary to write the following pathetic letter:—

To the LORD OF SOMERSET.

" It is now somewhat more than a year since I took the boldness to make my purpose of professing divinity known to your lordship, as to a person,

6

whom God had made so great an instrument of His providence in this kingdom, as that nothing in it should be done without your knowledge, your lordship exercised upon me then many of your virtues, for besides, that by your bounty I have lived ever since, it hath been through your lordship's advice, and inspiration of new hopes into me, that I have lived cheerfully. By this time, perchance, your lordship may have discerned that the malignity of my ill-fortune may infect your good, and that by some impressions in your lordship, I may be incapable of the favours which your lordship had purposed to me. . . . I humbly, therefore, beg of your lordship that, after you shall have been pleased to admit into your memory, that I am now a year older, broken with some sickness, and in the same degree of honesty as I was, your lordship will afford me one commandment, and bid me either hope for this business in your lordship's hand, or else pursue my first purpose, or abandon all, for as I cannot live without your favour so I cannot die without your leave; because even by dying, I should steal from you one, who is, by his own devotions and your purchase, your lordship's most humble and thankful servant."

Reading between the lines, it is evident that Rochester had made more than one attempt to serve his friend during the past year, but without success —the king was inexorable. Donne himself saw now that it was in vain to resist the Divine leading, and that he must return to the resolve from which he had been diverted, only to find more disappointment. This time he would not swerve.

And yet even now he found it impossible to break away from his surroundings. In spite of himself he was compelled to play the part of courtier, and to do the work of a court poet at the bidding of his patrons. From the moment when he had made up his mind to give himself up to the higher life and the service of the Church of Christ in the sanctuary, the hollowness of this wretched routine of amusement, and ceremony, and pomps, and vanities must have fretted his soul with a continual sense of emptiness. What a purposeless life he was leading! The world was just using him for its own ends, and what was he gaining by it all? God schools some men in one way, and some in another. Donne had to endure a very, very hard schooling. The closer we follow his career at this time, the sadder and more pitiful does it appear to a thoughtful reader.

On the 6th November of this year [1612] Prince Henry, the heir to the crown, died in his nineteenth year, after a short illness, to the sincere grief of the nation at large. He was buried in Westminster Abbey; and, among other tributes to his memory, Donne wrote an "Elegy upon the Untimely Death of the Incomparable Prince of Wales." It is not a successful performance, and among the least readable of his poems that have been preserved.

Two months later the Princess Elizabeth, the king's only daughter, was married to the Elector Frederick. Again Donne appears to have been ordered to write the "Epithalamium." The marriage was celebrated on the 15th February 1613, and the poet makes the most of the day, being St. Valentine's

Day.   The beautiful opening stanza sounds like an echo of Chaucer—

> " Hail, Bishop Valentine—whose day this is !
>   All the air is thy Diocese,
> And all the chirping choristers
> And other birds are thy parishioners.
>   Thou marriest, every year,
> The lyrick lark and the grave whispering dove ;
>   The sparrow that neglects his life for love,
> The household bird with the red stomacher ;
> Thou mak'st the blackbird speed as soon
>   As doth the goldfinch or the halcyon ;
>   The husband cock looks out, and straight is sped,
> And meets his wife, which brings her feather bed.
> This day more cheerfully than ever shine (!)
> This day, which might inflame thyself, Old Valentine ! "

Two months later we find him paying a visit to Sir Edward Herbert at Montgomery Castle.[1]

On the 3rd August he was at home again, for on that day a son, Nicholas, was baptized at St. Clement's in the Strand.   The remaining months of this year were rendered for ever memorable by the bad business of the divorce of Robert, Earl of Essex (afterwards General of the Parliamentary army), from his wife Frances, daughter of Thomas Howard, Earl of Suffolk, and her subsequent marriage to Lord Rochester on the 26th December.   Rochester was created Earl of Somerset three days before, that he might be placed in the same rank with his wife's relations—the Howards.[2]

---

[1] *Hist. MSS.* com. Rutland MSS., vol. ix. p. 6.

[2] The hideous exposure which followed less than two years later has cast a dreadful glare upon this shocking episode ; but no suspicion of what came to light afterwards seems to have been entertained by anyone at the time.   It is only fair to add that, while no one doubts

Again Donne was called upon to write the marriage song; it is a poor performance, and does him little credit. The wedding was celebrated at Whitehall: Montagu, Bishop of Bath and Wells, performed the ceremony; Dr. Mountaine, Dean of Westminster, preached the sermon; the bride's father gave her away; the king and queen, with the Archbishop of Canterbury, were present on the occasion. But Donne himself was not there; he had been struck down by a very serious illness, apparently of a typhoid character. In one of his letters at this time he describes himself as "more than half blind."

He had scarcely recovered from this severe attack when the death of Lady Bedford's brother (2nd Feb. 1614) induced him once more to court the muse. This time it was no task work, but an offering of sympathetic regret at the loss of one he had loved, besides being an attempt to console the noble lady who had befriended him so long. In the concluding lines of this elegy, as we have seen (chap. ii. p. 47), Donne pledged himself to write no more verse.

After the Somerset marriage we hear no more of any attempts to get State preferment. It is clear that Donne had by this time ceased to desire it; his mind was fully made up to embrace the sacred calling. When it became known that he had finally resolved to follow the king's original suggestion, his friends were unanimous in expressing their approval; and among them his old master, the Lord Keeper

that Lady Essex had compassed the death of Sir Thomas Overbury, the evidence against Somerset broke down; and, by the general verdict of legal experts, he stands acquitted of any knowledge of or complicity in the crime.

Egerton (now Lord Ellesmere) was foremost in sending
him kind assurances of his goodwill, and expressing
for him his strong regard.   Donne was much touched
by this and other such evidences of sympathy and
encouragement as came to him.   In a letter to
Sir Henry Wotton (?), who was then at Venice, he
hints, somewhat obscurely, that he had some hope of
paying his old friend a visit—there was now small
reason why he should not do so, and it might help
him to recover his shattered health.   Then he adds a
significant announcement: "But I must tell you in
the meantime that I have lately been in a long conference with a neighbour, and old friend of mine, who
was a companion to me in my first studies; and now
he will needs be giving me counsel.   And touching
the course which he advises me, I am not only of
opinion that it is best, but I had long since in mine
own judgment resolved upon it. . . . Believe me, I
do not cast into the account of my years, these last
five which I have lived [no] otherwise than as nights
slept out, which are indeed a part of *time*—which the
body steals from the mind, rather than a part of *life*,
which cannot live but it must feel itself alive.   God
Almighty awake me!   And in the meantime I think
that even this sleep I am in, is but a troubled one.
I have not forgotten that in a letter of yours you
asked me once, whether we should be fine gentlemen
still ?   In English, as I took it, whether still idlers,
without aims or ends ?   My mark is chosen, which I
would be infinitely glad might be also yours, as I am
yours."

The friend here alluded to is Dr. John King,
Bishop of London, who had been chaplain to the

Lord Keeper when Donne was his secretary. It is noticeable that Sir Henry Wotton, when at the end of his brilliant career as a diplomatist he became Provost of Eton, was himself ordained.

During the last eight or ten months of this year 1614 Donne was evidently living with his family at Drury House; he had given up his attendance at court, and was turning all his thoughts and all his studies in one direction. In his case there should be no lack of devout and earnest preparation for the new career upon which he was about to embark. It was during this time that he wrote those *Essays in Divinity* which his son published in 1651. " They were printed," we are told, " from an exact copy under the author's own hand, and were the voluntary sacrifices of several hours when he had many debates betwixt God and himself whether he were worthy and competently learned to enter into holy orders. They are now published both to testify his modest valuation of himself, and to show his great abilities; and they may serve to inform them in many holy curiosities."

The little 12mo volume of 224 pages is now extremely rare. No second edition appeared till the present writer reissued it, with a brief biographical preface and some editorial notes, in 1855. This edition, too, has long been out of print, and is now seldom to be met with. It must be confessed that the bookling is rather a literary curiosity than anything else. The essays were evidently never meant for publication. They are recorded soliloquies in which the writer sets himself to deal with perplexities and difficulties which presented themselves to his

own mind while giving himself to a critical study of
Holy Scripture. They read like entries in a diary, in
which one question after another is stated with only
a short hint or suggestion of the direction in which
inquiry might be pursued, but there is no attempt
at exhaustive treatment, little method, and little of
that close and severe reasoning that appears in the
Biathanatos or the *Pseudo Martyr*. Perhaps the best
impression that could be conveyed of the little volume
would be to call it a fragmentary collection of religious
exercises interspersed with devotions written down
from time to time with a view to utilise suggestions
and illustrations hereafter in the pulpit when his
work as a preacher should begin. The style is not
ornate or finished, the thoughts are often expressed
in language involved and rugged, as if the writer were
content with setting down a hint for himself and there
leaving it. The prayers are the outpourings of a
heart that was laying itself open to the Heavenly
Father, and had no fear that he could be misunderstood nor miss acceptance, though he should wrap up
his spiritual yearnings in words that were too weak
in the expression of his aspiration.

I incline to believe that many of Donne's religious
poems were written during this period. Though he had
promised Lady Bedford, after the death of her brother,
that he would write no more verse, he kept that
promise doubtless in the spirit, but not in the letter;
but there was no reason why he should not collect his
poems in a volume before he was ordained, and so
protect himself from that which was not only likely
to happen, but which actually did happen, later on,
when many ' fugitive pieces were attributed to him,

which he certainly never could have penned. For several years past his name had been associated with verses more or less frivolous; he had written Satires, Elegies, Songs, and Sonnets, which had passed from hand to hand among the courtiers and men of letters —and some few of them were not such as he would wish to be read and dwelt on by the pure and innocent. If they were ever to be printed, let them be printed while he was still a layman, not pirated to his discredit when he should have begun to exercise the high calling of a priest of Christ's Church.

Poetry in those days was not generally accepted as the legitimate language in which the soul might pour forth its nobler thoughts—its longings, its holier sorrows and regrets. George Herbert was now little more than at the beginning of his university career, and for many years after Donne's ordination was going through a very similar experience to that which had kept the elder man so long hanging about the court. A poet was under some suspicion of being a " worldling," just as in our own days a clergyman with any reputation for culture or learning outside the domain of homiletics or theology is too generally assumed to be at best half-hearted in his ministerial life. Be it as it may, Donne thought it became him now to break with the old life and all its lighter pursuits and amusements, and from this time he allowed himself none of that joyous relaxation which the writing of poetry might have afforded him. So, before he finally turned his back upon the old ways and habits, he was induced to print at his own expense a little volume of poems, which he appears to have given away to some favoured few among his most

valued friends. Of this he writes to Sir Henry
Goodere on the 14th December 1614.

" One thing now I must tell you; but so softly that
I am loth to hear myself, and so softly that if that
good lady (Lady Bedford) were in the room with you
and this letter, she might not hear. It is that I am
brought to a necessity of printing my poems, and
addressing them to my Lord Chamberlain. This I
mean to do forthwith; not for much public view, but
at mine own cost a few copies. . . . I must do this as
a *valediction to the world* before I take orders . . . and
I would be just to my written words to Lord Harrington to write nothing after that."

Of this privately printed volume not a single copy
is known to exist; it has absolutely disappeared.
The fact is the more to be regretted, because, when a
collected edition of his works was published by his
son in 1633, no attempt was made to place them in
chronological order, and it becomes a matter of great
difficulty to assign even an approximate date to those
which are the worthiest of our admiration. In the
later years of his life Donne certainly did think fit to
change his resolve of writing no more verse, and it
may be that at that time the influence of George
Herbert was upon him, and that he had seen and
read in MS. some of those beautiful poems, which the
saintly Nicholas Ferrar, as Herbert's executor, issued
immediately after Herbert's death at Bemerton, and
just two years after Donne himself had passed away.

.   .   .   .   .   .

Little more than a month after the printing of the
poems, and almost certainly on the Feast of the
Conversion of St. Paul—25th January 1615—a day

which thereafter he always kept as a day of special
memories, Donne was ordained by his old friend,
Dr. John King, Bishop of London, though where
the ordination was held we have not been told, nor
does it seem likely that it will ever be discovered.
In February it was rumoured that he had been
appointed chaplain to the king. In point of fact, he
did not actually receive this appointment till nearly a
year later. On the 14th March he received, during
the royal progress at Cambridge, the degree of Doctor
of Divinity from the university, not, however, without
some protest from some members of the Theological
Faculty, who did not approve that an *Oxford man*
should be forced upon them for the highest academic
distinction which the university could confer. It
was on this occasion that his friend, Lord Hay, presented him with his doctor's robes.

CHAPTER IV

A BUNDLE OF LETTERS

A COLLECTION of letters of Dr. Donne was issued in a 4to volume by his son John, in 1654, that is, twenty-three years after his death. It was, as far as I know, the first collection of private letters ever published in England. The appearance of the volume, which had a large sale, was due to the high reputation which, during his lifetime, Donne had earned as a letter-writer. He was so much the representative man of letters of his time that his contemporaries valued and admired everything he wrote: for them, even his lighter writings had a peculiar charm which it is difficult for us to understand. Nevertheless, these letters tell us so much that he only could tell, —and could only tell in his own way,—they give us such a curious insight into fashions and ways of living, and *the tone of feeling* among the upper classes of society during the reign of James I., and they tell us so much, too, about the private life of the writer himself, and of the difficulties through which he passed, and the subtile questionings which helped him to " beat his music out," that it would be an injustice to him if a selection from his early correspondence did not form a part of this biography.

Donne's letters, of which about a hundred and sixty have come down to us, have never yet been edited with any care.

Those which are here printed, were written, with one single exception, before his ordination. I have arranged them in chronological order, by the help of such internal evidence as they severally afford. Donne was a little uncertain in dating his letters; at any-rate, among those which his son printed, only a fraction are fully dated, and this must make it difficult to determine even the year to which any one of them is to be referred. Happily, our sources for the history of the reign of James I. are very numerous; and if a letter deals at all with con-temporary events, a clue is rarely wanting.

I.

[DONNE *to* SIR HENRY GOODERE.][1]

" SIR,—Though you escape my lifting up of your latch by removing, you cannot my letters; yet of this letter I do not much accuse myself, for I serve your commandment in it, for it is only to convey to you this paper opposed to those, with which you trusted me. It is, I cannot say the weightiest, but truly the saddest lucubration and night's passage that ever I had. For it exercised those hours, which—with extreme danger of her, whom I should hardly have abstained from recompensing for her company in this world, with accompanying her out of it—increased my poor family with a son. Though her anguish,

[1] The date is January 1607. The son named is Francis, baptized at Micham on the 8th of that month.

and my fears, and hopes, seem divers and wild distractions from this small business of your papers, yet because they all narrowed themselves, and met in *via regia*, which is the consideration of ourselves and God, I thought it time not unfit for this dispatch. Thus much more than needed I have told you, whilst my fire was lighting at Tricombs, 10 o'clock.

"Yours ever entirely,

"J. DONNE."

II.

To the same.

"SIR,—In the history or style of friendship, which is best written both in deeds and words, a letter which is of a mixed nature, and hath something of both, is a mixed parenthesis: it may be left out, yet it contributes, thought not to the being, yet to the verdure, and freshness thereof. Letters have truly the same office, as oaths. As these amongst light and empty men, are but fillings, and pauses, and interjections; but with weightier, they are sad attestations; so are letters, to some compliment, and obligation to others. For mine, as I never authorised my servant to lie in my behalf (for if it were officious in him, it might be worse in me), so I allow my letters much less that civil dishonesty, both because they go from me more considerately, and because they are permanent; for in them I may speak to you in your chamber a year hence, before I know not whom, and not hear myself. They shall therefore ever keep the sincerity and intemerateness of the fountain, whence they are derived. And as wheresoever these leaves fall, the root is in my heart, so shall they, as that sucks good affections towards you there, have ever true impressions thereof. Thus much information is in very leaves, that they can tell what the tree is, and these can tell you I am a friend, and an honest man. Of what general use, the fruit should speak, and I have none: and of what particular profit to you, your application and experimenting should tell you, and you can make none of such a nothing; yet even of barren sycamores, such as I, there were use, if either any light flashings, or scorching vehemencies, or sudden showers made you need so shadowy an example or remembrancer. But (sir) your fortune and mind do you this happy injury, that they make all kinds of fruits useless unto you; therefore I have placed my love wisely where I need communicate nothing. All this, though perchance you read it not till Michaelmas, was told you at Micham, 15th August, 1607."

III.

To the same.

" SIR,—This letter hath more merit, than one of more diligence, for I wrote it in my bed, and with much pain. I have occasion to sit late some nights in my study (which your books make a pretty library), and now I find that that room hath a wholesome emblematic use: for having under it a vault, I make that promise me, that I shall die reading, since my book and a grave are so near. But it hath another as unwholesome, that by raw vapours rising from thence (for I can impute it to nothing else), I have contracted a sickness which I cannot name nor describe. For it hath so much of a continual cramp, that wrests the sinews, so much of a tetane, that it withdraws and pulls the mouth, and so much of the gout (which they whose counsel I use, say it is), that it is not like to be cured, though I am too hasty in three days to pronounce it. If it be the gout, I am miserable; for that affects dangerous parts, as my neck and breast, and (I think fearfully) my stomach, but it will not kill me yet; I shall be in this world, like a porter in a great house, ever nearest the door, but seldomest abroad: I shall have many things to make me weary, and yet not get leave to be gone. If I go, I will provide by my best means that you suffer not for me, in your bonds. The estate which I should leave behind me of any estimation, is my poor fame in the memory of my friends, and therefore I would be curious of it, and provide that they repent not to have loved me. Since my imprisonment in my bed, I have made a meditation in verse, which I call a "Litany"; the word you know imports no other than supplication, but all churches have one form of supplication, by that name. Amongst ancient annals, I mean some eight hundred years, I have met two Litanies in Latin verse, which gave me not the reason of my meditations, for in good faith I thought not upon them then, but they give me a defence, if any man, to a layman, and a private, impute it as a fault, to take such divine and public names, to his own little thoughts. The first of these was made by Ratpetus, a monk of Suevia; and the other by St. Notker, of whom I will give you this note by the way, that he is a private saint, for a few parishes; they were both but monks, and the Litanies poor and barbarous enough; yet Pope Nicholas V. valued their devotion so much, that he canonised both their poems, and commanded them for public service in their churches: mine is for lesser chapels, which are my friends, and though a copy of it were due to you, now, yet I am so unable to serve myself with writing it for you at this time (being some thirty staves of nine lines), that I must entreat you to take a promise that you shall have the first, for a testimony of that duty which I owe to your love, and to myself, who am bound to cherish it by my best offices. That by which it will deserve best acceptation, is, that neither the Roman Church need call it defective, because it abhors not the particular mention of the blessed triumphers in heaven; nor the Reformed can discreetly accuse it of attributing more than a rectified devotion ought to do. The day before I lay down, I was at London, where I delivered your letter to Sir Edward Conway, and received another for you, with the copy of my book, of which it is impossible for me to give you a copy so soon, for it is not of much less than three hundred pages. If I die, it shall come to you in that fashion that your letter desires it. If I warm again (as I have often seen such beggars as my indisposition is, end themselves soon, and the patient as soon), you and I shall speak together of that, before it be too late to serve you in that commandment. At this time I only assure you, that I have not appointed it upon any person, nor ever purposed to print it: which latter perchance you thought, and grounded your request thereupon.

A gentleman that visited me yesterday, told me that
our Church hath lost Mr. Hugh Broughton, who is
gone to the Roman side.   I have known before, that
Serarius the Jesuit, was an instrument from Cardinal
Baronius to draw him to Rome, to accept a stipend,
only to serve the Christian Churches in controversies
with the Jews, without endangering himself to change
of his persuasion in particular deductions between
these Christian Churches, or being inquired of, or
tempted thereunto.   And I hope he is no otherwise
departed from us.   If he be, we shall not escape
scandal in it; because, though he be a man of many
distempers, yet when he shall come to eat assured
bread, and to be removed from partialities—to which
want drove him, to make himself a reputation and
raise up favourers—you shall see in that course of
opposing the Jews, he will produce worthy things:
and our Church will perchance blush to have lost a
soldier fit for that great battle; and to cherish only
those single duellisms, between Rome and England,
or that more single, and almost self-homicide, between
the unconformed ministers, and bishops.   Sir, you
would pity me if you saw me write, and therefore
will pardon me if I write no more: my pain hath
drawn my head so much awry, and holds it so, that
mine eye cannot follow mine hand: I receive you
therefore into my prayers, with mine own weary
soul, and commend myself to yours.   I doubt not
but next week I shall be good news to you, for I
have mending or dying on my side, which is two to
one.   If I continue thus, I shall have comfort in
this, that my blessed Saviour exercising His justice
upon my two worldly parts, my fortune, and body,

reserves all His mercy for that which best tastes it,
and most needs it, my soul.   I profess to you truly,
that my lothness to give over now, seems to myself
an ill sign that I shall write no more.

"Your poor friend, and God's poor patient,

"J. DONNE."

The mention of Hugh Broughton, as having "gone
to the Roman side," fixes the date of this letter.
Broughton, of whom a fair account is given in the
Dictionary of National Biography, never had any
dream of "going to the Roman side"; but he left
England in 1607, and returned only to die in 1611.
The letter is interesting as showing that, however ill
he may have been, it was Donne's practice to write
on his sickbed.   The book referred to can be none
other than the *Biathanatos*.

IV.

A. V. MERCED.[1]

"SIR,—I write not to you out of my poor library,
where to cast mine eye upon good authors kindles or
refreshes sometimes meditations not unfit to communicate to near friends; nor from the high way,
where I am contracted, and inverted into myself;
which are my two ordinary forges of letters to you,
but I write from the fireside of my parlour, and in
the noise of three gamesome children; and by the
side of her, whom because I have transplanted into
a wretched fortune, I must labour to disguise that

---

[1] *A vuestra merced,* a Spanish compliment signifying, *to your
worship,* or *your grace.*

from her by all such honest devices, as giving her my
company and discourse, therefore I steal from her,
all the time which I give this letter, and it is therefore that I take so short a list, and gallop so fast
over it. I have not been out of my house since I
received your packet. As I have much quenched
my senses and disused my body from pleasure, and
so tried how I can endure to be mine own grave, so
I try now how I can suffer a prison. And since it
is but to build one wall more about our soul, she is
still in her own centre how many circumferences soever
fortune or our own perverseness cast about her. I
would I could as well entreat her to go out, as she
knows whither to go. But if I melt into a melancholy whilst I write, I shall be taken in the manner:
and I sit by one too tender towards these impressions,
and it is so much our duty, to avoid all occasions of
giving them sad apprehensions, as St. Hierome accuses
Adam of no other fault in eating the apple, but that
he did it *Ne contristaretur delicias suas.* I am not
careful what I write, because the enclosed letters
may dignify this ill-favoured bark, and they need not
grudge so coarse a countenance because they are now
to accompany themselves; my man fetched them,
and therefore I can say no more of them than
themselves say; Mistress Meautys entreated me by
her letter to hasten hers, as I think, for by my troth
I cannot read it. My lady was dispatching in so
much haste for Twickenham, as she gave no word to
a letter which I sent with yours; of Sir Thomas
Bartlet, I can say nothing, nor of the plague, though
your letter bid me: but that he diminishes, the
other increases, but in what proportion I am not

clear. To them at Hammersmith, and Mrs. Herbert
I will do your command. If I have been good in
hope, or can promise any little offices in the future,
probably it is comfortable, for I am the worst present
man in the world; yet the instant, though it be
nothing, joins times together, and therefore this
unprofitableness, since I have been, and will still
endeavour to be so, shall not interrupt me now from
being

" Your servant and lover,

" J. DONNE."

Mistress Meautys is Jane, daughter of Hercules
Meautys, Esq., of West Ham, County Essex. She was
one of the young ladies who "waited on" Lady
Bedford. She married Sir William Cornwallis of
Brome, County Suffolk, in 1608.

V.

To the same.

" SIR,—Though my friendship be good for nothing
else, it may give you the profit of a tentation, or of
an affliction: it may excuse your patience; and
though it cannot allure it shall importune you.
Though I know you have many worthy friends of all
ranks, yet I add something, since I which am of none,
would fain be your friend too. There is some of the
honour and some of the degree of a creation, to make
a friendship of nothing. Yet, not to annihilate myself
utterly (for though it seem humbleness, yet it is a
work of as much almightiness to bring a thing to
nothing, as from nothing), though I be not of the

best stuff for friendship, which men of warm and
durable fortunes only are, I cannot say that I am
not of the best fashion, if truth and honesty be that;
which I must ever exercise, towards you, because I
learned it of you: for the conversation with worthy
men and of good example though it sow not virtue
in us, yet produceth and ripeneth it. Your man's
haste, and mine to Micham, cuts off this letter here,
yet, as in little patterns torn from a whole piece, this
may tell you what all I am. Though by taking me
before my day (which I accounted Tuesday) I make
short payment of this duty of letters, yet I have a
little comfort in this, that you see me hereby willing
to pay those debts which I can, before my time.

"Your affectionate friend,

"J. Donne.

"First Saturday in March 1607 [i.e. 7th March 1608.]

"You forgot to send me the Apology; and many
times, I think it an injury to remember one of a
promise, lest it confess a distrust. But of the book,
by occasion of reading the Dean's answer to it, I
have sometimes some want."

The book mentioned is Brerely's *The Protestant
Apologie for the Roman Church*; the real author of
which work was Lawrence Anderton, S.J. The book
was published in London in 1606. Dr. Morton's
answer to Brerely was presented to James I. on the
27th October 1609. It is clear, from this letter,
that Donne was at this time "reading"—i.e. *revising,
correcting and suggesting*—for Morton's *Catholic Appeale*,
which was at this time being prepared for the press;
"the Dean" is, of course, Dr. Morton.

VI.

To the same.

" SIR,—To you that are not easily scandalized, and in whom, I hope, neither my religion nor morality can suffer, I dare write my opinion of that book in whose bowels you left me. It hath refreshed, and given new justice to my ordinary complaint, that the divines of these times, are become mere advocates, as though religion were a temporal inheritance; they plead for it with all sophistications, and illusions, and forgeries, and herein are they likest advocates, that though they be feed by the way with dignities, and other recompenses, yet that for which they plead is none of theirs. They write for religion, without it. In the main point in question, I think truly there is a perplexity (as far as I see yet), and both sides may be in justice and innocence ; and the wounds which they inflict upon the adverse part, are all *se defendendo*: for, clearly, our state cannot be safe without the oath ; since they profess, that clergymen, though traitors, are no subjects, and that all the rest may be none to-morrow. And, as clearly, the supremacy which the Roman Church pretends, were diminished, if it were limited ; and will as ill abide that, or disputation, as the prerogative of temporal kings, who being the only judges of their prerogative, why may not Roman bishops (so enlightened as they are presumed by them) be good witnesses of their own supremacy, which is now so much impugned ? But for this particular author, I looked for more prudence, and human wisdom in him,

in avoiding all miscitings, or misinterpretings, because
at this time, the watch is set, and everybody's hammer
is upon that anvil; and to dare offend in that kind
now is, for a thief to leave the covert, and meet a
strong hue and cry in the teeth: and yet truly this
man is extremely obnoxious in that kind; for, though
he have answered many things fully (as no book ever
gave more advantage than that which he undertook),
and abound in delicate applications, and ornaments,
from the divine and profane authors, yet being chiefly
conversant about two points, he prevaricates in both.
For, for the matter, which is the first, he refers it
entirely, and namely, to that which Dr. Morton hath
said therein before, and so leaves it roundly: and for
the person (which is the second) upon whom he
amasses as many opprobries, as any other could
deserve, he pronounceth, that he will account any
answer from his adversary, slander, except he do (as
he hath done) draw whatsoever he saith of him, from
authors of the same religion, and in print: and so, he
having made use of all the quodlibetaries and imputa-
tions against the other, cannot be obnoxious himself
in that kind, and so hath provided safely.   It were
no service to you, to send you my notes upon the
book, because they are sandy, and incoherent rags,
for my memory, not for your judgment; and to
extend them to an easiness, and perspicuity, would
make them a pamphlet, not a letter.   I will therefore
defer them till I see you; and in the meantime, I
will adventure to say to you, without inserting one
unnecessary word, that the book is full of falsifications
in words and in sense, and of falsehoods in matter of
fact, and of inconsequent and unscholarlike arguings,

and of relinquishing the king, in many points of defence, and of contradiction of himself, and of dangerous and suspected doctrine in divinity, and of silly ridiculous triflings, and of extreme flatteries, and of neglecting better and more obvious answers, and of letting slip some enormous advantages which the other gave, and he spies not. I know (as I begun) I speak to you who cannot be scandalized, and that neither measure religion (as it is now called) by unity, nor suspect unity, for these interruptions. Sir, not only a mathematic point, which is the most indivisible and unique thing which art can present, flows into every line which is derived from the centre, but our soul which is but one, hath swallowed up a negative, and feeling soul; which was in the body before it came, and exercises those faculties yet; and God Himself, who only is one, seems to have been eternally delighted, with a disunion of persons. They whose active function it is, must endeavour this unity in religion: and we at our lay altars (which are our tables, or bedside, or stools, wheresoever we dare prostrate ourselves to God in prayer) must beg it of Him : but we must take heed of making misconclusions upon the want of it : for, whether the mayor and alderman fall out (as with us and the Puritans; bishops against priests), or the commoners' voices differ who is mayor, and who alderman, or what their jurisdiction (as with the Bishop of Rome, or whosoever), yet it is still one corporation.

"Your very affectionate servant and lover,

"Micham, Thursday, late. "J. DONNE."

"Never leave the remembrance of my poor service unmentioned when you see the good lady."

The severe and trenchant criticism in this letter was provoked by Bishop William Barlow's *Answer to a Catholike Englishman*, dedicated to James I., and published in a 4to volume of 370 pages, in 1609. It is a wretched performance; but Barlow had, all his life through, some very zealous friends, and he must have had some popular talents.

VII.

To Yourself.

"SIR,—All your other letters, which came to me by more hazardous ways, had therefore much merit in them; but for your letter by Mr. Pory, it was but a little degree of favour, because the messenger was so obvious, and so certain, that you could not choose but write by him. But since he brought me as much letter as all the rest, I must accept that, as well as the rest.

"By this time, Mr. Garret, when you know in your conscience that you have sent no letter, you begin to look upon the superscription, and doubt that you have broken up some other body's letter: but whose soever it were is must speak the same language, for I have heard from nobody.

"Sir, if there be a proclamation in England against writing to me, yet since it is thereby become a matter of state, you might have told Mr. Pory so. And you might have told him, what became of Sir Thomas Lucy's letter, in my first packet (for any letter to him makes any paper a packet, and any piece of single money a medal), and what became of my Lady Kingsmel's in my second, and of hers in my third whom I will not name to you in hope that it is perished, and you lost the honour of giving it.

"Sir, mine own desire of being your servant, hath sealed me a patent of that place during my life, and therefore it shall not be in the power of your forbidding (to which your stiff silence amounts) to make me leave being

"Your very affectionate servant,
"J. DONNE."

This letter was written to George Gerrard, second son of Sir William Gerrard [Garrard or Garret] of Dorney, County Bucks. He was an early and life-long friend of Donne's, and became Master of the Charterhouse.

Donne was at this time abroad with Sir Robert Drury, and looking for letters from his friends. None, it seems, had reached him. Mr. Pory was a king's messenger who went to and fro with despatches. Sir Thomas Lucy was the son and heir of Sir Thomas Lucy of Charlcote, whose deer Shakespeare is said to have had to do with. He had travelled with Lord Herbert of Cherbury in 1608-9, and was a close friend of Donne's.

VIII.

To the Honourable Knight, SIR ROBERT CARR,
Gentleman of His Highness's Bedchamber.

"SIR,—I have always your leave to use my liberty, but now I must use my bondage. Which is my necesssity of obeying a precontract laid upon me. I go to-morrow to Camberwell, a mile beyond South-

wark. But from this town goes with me my brother
Sir Thomas Grymes and his lady, and I with them.
There we dine well enough I warrant you, with his
father-in-law, Sir Thomas Hunt. If I keep my whole
promise, I shall preach both forenoon and afternoon.
But I will obey your commandments for my return.
If you cannot be there by ten, do not put yourself
upon the way: for, sir, you have done me more
honour, than I can be worthy of, in missing me so
diligently. I can hope to hear Mr. Moulin again:
or ruminate what I have heretofore heard. The only
miss that I shall have is of the honour of waiting upon
you; which is somewhat recompensed, if thereby you
take occasion of not putting yourself to that pain, to
be more assured of the inabilities of

" Your unworthy servant,

" J. DONNE."

Internal evidence shows this letter to have been
written within six months after Donne's ordination.
Peter du Moulin, the French divine, preached before
James I. on the 6th June 1615. He had been
invited to England by the king, but his stay was
short. Sir Thomas Hunt of Foulsham, Norfolk,
married, as his second wife, Jane, mother of Sir
Thomas Grymes of Camberwell. He himself died in
January 1617. Donne was evidently engaged to
preach twice at Camberwell.

CHAPTER V

LINCOLN'S INN DAYS

IZAAK WALTON tells us that Donne preached his first sermon in the parish church of Paddington, then a village on the outskirts of London. The living was a "perpetual curacy" in the gift of the Bishop of London, and the incumbent was one Griffen Edwards, of whom little is known. He had held Paddington with the curacy of Marylebone since 1598, and continued to hold them till 1640. We can well believe that he was glad to offer his pulpit to one who was already famous and marked out for high preferment. The little church, though it had an east window filled with stained glass, in which a figure of St. Catherine occupied the most conspicuous place, must have been already in a condition of decay, and about sixty years later,—in 1678,—being old and ruinous, it was pulled down and rebuilt at the cost of Sir Joseph—Lord Mayor of London in 1675—and his brother, Mr. Daniel Shelton, the lessee of the manor of Paddington. What the subject of Donne's sermon was we are not told.

The earliest dated sermon which has come down to us was preached before Queen Anne of Denmark at Greenwich, on the 30th April. The queen was at this time spending large sums of money upon this her

favourite residence, under the direction and advice of
Inigo Jones, and had gone there from Somerset House,
afterwards better known as Denmark House, which
was her town residence.   Here, just a week previously,
Villiers had been knighted by the king, after being
made a Gentleman of the Bedchamber.   Lord Somerset was playing his cards very badly, and his influence
with James was almost gone.   Villiers had entirely
supplanted him.   And though he was now only in his
twenty-third year, he was rising every day in his royal
master's favour, and treated by that master rather as
a son than as a subject.   The text of Donne's sermon
on this occasion was taken from Isaiah lii. 3 : " *Thus
saith the Lord, Ye have sold yourselves for nought ; and
ye shall be redeemed without money.*"   Donne seems to
have set himself in his sermon to lift up his voice
against the portentous extravagance of his time. Seldom in our history has there been more reckless squan-
derings and senseless profusion than in the days of
James I.   Donne's warm friend, Lord Hay, was conspicuous for the unmeasured waste of his large resources,
and the mischievous example which he set of costly
entertainments and magnificent display.   On the
other hand, the fashion of leaving money and lands
for charitable uses—after having gone out since the
spoliation of the monasteries for well-nigh a century—
had now begun to revive, and was soon to be signalised
by such foundations as that of the Charterhouse by
Sutton, and of Dulwich College by Allen.   It is
worthy of notice how Donne so early in his career
sets himself to deal with this subject.

"God can raise up children out of the stones of
the street," he says, " and therefore He might be as

liberal as He would of His people, and suffer them to be sold for old shoes. But Christ will not sell His birthright for a mess of pottage, the kingdom of heaven for the dole at a funeral. Heaven is not to be had in exchange for an hospital, or a chantry, or a college erected in thy last will; it is not only the selling of all we have, that must buy that pearl, which represents the kingdom of heaven; the giving of all that we have to the poor, at our death, will not do it; the pearl must be sought, and found before, in an even and constant course of sanctification; we must be thrifty all our life, or we shall be too poor for that purchase."

How the preacher was listened to we are not told: the probability is that the man who so lately had been conspicuous among the courtiers as a wit and man of letters would hardly be accepted thus early as a pulpit orator with a message from God. Curiosity must have been uppermost in the minds of his hearers, and the thought, "Is Saul also among the prophets?" He had to win confidence and respect, and it seems that he did not take the town by storm.

During the year which passed after his ordination we hear little or nothing of his movements. Walton's assertion that he received the offer of fourteen benefices during this short period is quite incredible, and the other assertion that immediately after his ordination the king made him his chaplain is certainly untrue.

More than a year later he writes to Lord Hay, begging him to use his influence to obtain this distinction for him.

It seems clear that James, after obtaining for him

the doctor's degree at Cambridge, had not thought fit
to do anything more for him until he had had some
probation and shown himself qualified for preferment.
Donne was saddened, and entreated Lord Hay " to
take some time to move His Majesty before he go out
of town, that I may be his servant, which request
. . . I hope you shall not find difficult nor unreason-
able." The application was made accordingly, and on
the 21st April 1616 we find Donne preaching at
Whitehall just at the time when the horrible revela-
tions connected with the murder of Sir Thomas Overbury were being discussed by everyone and were the
subject of common talk. The sermon on Eccles. viii.
11—" *Because sentence against an evil work is not executed speedily, therefore the heart of the sons of men is fully
set in them to do evil* "—contains some fine passages
which the congregation can hardly have helped applying to the dreadful circumstances uppermost in the
minds of all ; and the text itself must have come upon
them with a profound suggestiveness and significance.

A little after this, Donne was presented to the
living of Keystone in Hunts, and in July he became
rector of the valuable benefice of Sevenoaks in Kent.
At neither of these places did he ever reside for more
than a few weeks at a time, though he held the first
till 1622, and the other to the end of his life.

In those days the holder of a benefice was considered
to have done his duty to the parish from which he
derived his income, if he took due care that the
ordinary ministrations of divine service in the
sanctuary were adequately provided for, and the
parsonage occupied by a curate who ministered to the
necessities and spiritual wants of the people. There

was no feeling against a man of learning and eminence holding two or more livings in plurality. It was thought better that a clergyman of great gifts should be supported out of the surplus income of a rich benefice, and allowed to exercise his talents in a sphere which needed his personal presence and influence, rather than that he should be buried in a country village where he would be likely to live and die forgotten and unknown.

In the autumn of this year (1616) another piece of preferment was offered to and accepted by Donne. The Preachership of Lincoln's Inn, then regarded as one of the most important positions which a clergyman could hold in London, fell vacant by the death of Dr. Thomas Holloway, Fellow of Balliol, who had held it since 1611. Donne had many friends among the Benchers, not the least zealous being Christopher Brooke, who had got himself into trouble by being present at Donne's marriage. By an order of the Masters of the Bench, dated 24th October 1616, it was resolved that "Mr. Doctor Donne is at this council chosen to be Divinity Reader of this house, . . . and is to preach every Sabbath day in the term, both forenoon and afternoon, and once before and after every term, and on the grand days every forenoon, and on the reading times." The post was no sinecure; it involved the preaching of about fifty sermons every year to a highly-educated and critical audience. "And now," says Walton, "his life was as a shining light among his old friends; now he gave ocular testimony of the strictness and regularity of it; now he might say, as St. Paul adviseth the Corinthians, *' Be ye followers of me, as I follow Christ, and walk as*

8

ye have me for an example,' not the example of a busy-
body, but of a contemplative, a harmless, a humble,
and a holy life and conversation."

To Donne the appointment was in every way a
desirable one; " for, besides fair lodgings that were set
apart and newly furnished for him with all necessaries,
other courtesies were also daily added, indeed, so
many and so freely, as if they meant their gratitude
should exceed his merits,—he preaching faithfully and
constantly to them, and they liberally rewarding him."

After long years of waiting and difficulty, prosperity
had come at last. He was now in his forty-third
year, and, if his income was not too large, it was, at
anyrate, sufficient for his necessities, and his time of
anxiety was at an end.

While Donne had been living for the last sixteen
years the anxious and worrying life of a man whose
income could never be made to square with his
necessary expenditure, his mother, who had been left
in affluence at her first husband's death, in 1575, had
herself experienced great vicissitudes of fortune.

We know very little about her during those years;
there is no doubt that she was a zealous and profuse
supporter of the seminary priests and Jesuit fathers,
and that she was noted as a liberal contributor to the
necessities of those who, like herself, were determined
adherents of the " Catholic " persuasion. A lady,
whose portion bequeathed by her first husband was
considerable, was not likely to remain long a widow.
It is true she had six children, but they too were all
provided for, and she can hardly have been thirty
years old when her first husband died. The books of
the Ironmongers' Company show that all her children

died under age except the future Dean of St. Paul's, and a daughter, Anne, who in 1586 married Avery Copeley, one of a Yorkshire family—all of whom were staunch Romanists, and many of them suffered for their religious opinions. In 1594 Anne married, as her second husband, William Lyly of London, gentleman, of whom I have discovered nothing. She appears to have died about 1616. Her mother had by this time changed her name, at least once, since her first widowhood,[1] and had, as we must infer from her son's letter addressed to her in her hour of sorrow and bereavement, spent all her own fortune.

The following letter acquires a peculiar interest and pathos when it is remembered that something like estrangement between mother and son must inevitably have arisen in consequence of the decided line which Donne had taken in the religious discussions of the time, and the consequent cleavage that had ensued in what had been common ground for mother and son in earlier days.

Though this letter is undated, it is certain that it was written before the 15th August 1617, when Donne lost his wife.

DR. DONNE *to his* MOTHER, *comforting her after the death of her daughter.*

"MY MOST DEAR MOTHER,—When I consider so much of your life, as can fall within my memory and

---

[1] My lamented friend, the late T. R. O'fflahertie, professed to have discovered a second and third marriage of Donne's mother—the second to one Simmonds, the third to a Mr. Rainsford. He could tell me nothing about either of them.

observation, I find it to have been a sea, under a
continual tempest, where one wave hath ever over-
taken another. Our most wise and blessed Saviour
chooseth what way it pleaseth Him, to conduct those
which He loves to His haven and eternal rest. The
way which He hath chosen for you is strait, stormy,
obscure, and full of sad apparitions of death and wants,
and sundry discomforts; and it hath pleased Him,
that one discomfort should still succeed, and touch
another, that He might leave you no leisure, by any
pleasure or abundance, to stay or step out of that way,
or almost to take breath in that way by which He
hath determined to bring you home, which is His
glorious kingdom. One of the most certain marks
and assurances, that all these are His works, and to
that good end is your inward feeling and apprehension
of them a patience in them. As long as the Spirit
of God distils and dews His cheerfulness upon your
heart; as long as He instructs your understanding to
interpret His mercies and His judgments aright; so
long your comfort must needs be as much greater than
others as your afflictions are greater than theirs. The
happiness which God afforded to your first young
time; which was the love and care of my most dear
and provident father, whose soul, I hope hath long
since enjoyed the sight of our blessed Saviour, and had
compassion of all our miseries in the world, God
removed from you quickly, and hath since taken
from you all the comfort that that marriage produced.
All those children (for whose maintenance his industry
provided, and for whose education you were so carefully and so chargeably diligent) He hath now taken
from you. All that wealth which he left, God hath

suffered to be gone from us all; so that God hath
seemed to repent, that He allowed any part of your life
any earthly happiness; that He might keep your soul
in continual exercise, and longing, and assurance of
coming immediately to Him. I hope therefore, my
most dear mother, that your experience of the
calamities of this life, your continual acquaintance with
the visitations of the Holy Ghost, which gives better
inward comforts, than the world can outward discomforts, your wisdom to distinguish the value of this
world from the next, and your religious fear of
offending our merciful God by repining at anything
which He doeth, will preserve you from any inordinate
and dangerous sorrow for the loss of my most beloved
sister. For my part, which am only left now to do
the office of a child, though the poorness of my
fortune, and the greatness of my charge, hath not
suffered me to express my duty towards you, as became
me; yet I protest to you before Almighty God and His
angels and saints in heaven, that I do, and ever shall,
esteem myself to be as strongly bound to look to you
and provide for your relief, as for my own poor wife
and children. For whatsoever I shall be able to do
I acknowledge to be a debt to you from whom I had
that education, which must make my fortune. This I
speak not as though I feared my father Rainsford's
care of you, or his means to provide for you; for he
hath been with me, and I perceive in him a loving and
industrious care to give you contentment, so, I see in
his business a happy and considerable forwardness.
In the meantime, good mother, take heed that no
sorrow nor dejection in your heart interrupt or
disappoint God's purpose in you; His purpose is to

remove out of your heart all such love of this world's
happiness as might put Him out of possession of it.
He will have you entirely, and as God is comfort
enough, so He is inheritance enough.   Join with God
and make His visitations and afflictions as He intended
them, mercies and comforts.   And for God's sake
pardon those negligences which I have heretofore used
towards you; and assist me with your blessing to me,
and all mine; and with your prayers to our blessed
Saviour, that thereby both my mind and fortune may
be apt to do all my duties, especially those that belong
to you.

"God, whose omnipotent strength can change the
nature of anything by His raising-spirit of comfort,
make your poverty riches, your afflictions pleasure, and
all the gall and wormwood of your life honey and
manna to your taste which He hath wrought whensoever you are willing to have it so.   Which, because I
cannot doubt in you, I will forbear more lines at this
time, and most humbly deliver myself over to your
devotions and good opinion of me, which I desire no
longer to live than I may have."

.   .   .   .   .   .

Only fourteen sermons preached at Lincoln's Inn
have come down to us.   They were probably those
which Donne himself prepared for the press before his
death, thinking them such as were worth preserving
and handing down to posterity.

Donne was no mere rhetorician—he practised none
of those arts which charm the multitude.   Even at
St. Dunstan's, in his fully-written sermons, he seems
to be always addressing himself to men of thought,
refinement, and culture.   These were the men among

whom he had lived from his boyhood; he knew them well, their weaknesses, their temptations, their vices, their regrets, their rivalries, their ambitions; he had lived in sympathy with those who had been disappointed, and those who had gone astray, and those who had the battle to fight in the upper walks of social life, and he knew that among them too there were souls saddened by a sense of sin, troubled by doubts and questionings, finding it very hard to be pure and true; and yet there were among them many who were stretching forth lame hands of faith, and seeking after a closer walk with God in circumstances from which they could not hope to escape, and under the pressure of which to live the higher life was very, very hard. It was to these, and such as these, that Donne's earlier sermons are addressed; he never tried to *preach down* to his congregation—the greatest of all mistakes for any man to make who hopes to raise others. Sometimes, but not often, Donne rather falls into the other extreme of seeming to apologise for taking too high a stand. But at Lincoln's Inn he is always direct, outspoken, fearless, and his words must have come home to many who heard him. Take the following as a specimen of his most familiar manner :—

" I am not all here. I am here now preaching upon this text; and I am at home in my library considering whether St. Gregory, or St. Hierome, have said best of this text before. I am here speaking to you, and yet I consider by the way, in the same instant what it is likely you will say to one another, when I have done. You are not all here neither, you are here now, hearing me, and yet you are thinking that you have heard a better sermon, somewhere else on this text before. You are here, and yet you think you could have heard some other doctrine of downright predestination, and reprobation roundly delivered somewhere else with more edification to you. You are here, and you remember yourselves that now ye think of it, this had been the fittest time—now when everybody else is at church, to have made such and such a private visit, and because you would be there you are there."

Here is another characteristic passage—

" The whole need not a physician, but the sick do. If you mistake yourself to be well, or think you have physic enough at home, knowledge enough, divinity enough, to save you without us, you need no physician, that is a physician can do you no good, but then is this God's physic, and God's physician welcome unto you if you become to a remorseful sense, and to an humble and penitent acknowledgment that you are sick, and that there is no soundness in your flesh because of His anger, nor any rest in your bones, because of your sins, till you turn upon Him in whom this anger is appeased, and in whom these sins are forgiven, the Son of His love, the Son of His right hand, at His right hand Christ Jesus."

The following affords a good example of Donne's more conversational style :—

" But whilst we are in the consideration of this arch, this roof of separation, between God and us, by sin, there may be use in imparting to you an observation, a passage of mine own.

" Lying at Aix, at Aquisgrane, a well-known town in Germany, and fixing there some time for the benefit of

those baths, I found myself in a house which was divided
into many families, and indeed so large as it might
have been a little parish, or at least a great limb of a
great one; but it was of no parish, for when I asked
who lay over my head, they told me a family of Anabaptists. And who over theirs? Another family of
Anabaptists; and another family of Anabaptists over
theirs, and the whole house was a nest of these boxes,
several artificers, all Anabaptists. I asked in what
room they met for the exercise of their religion, I
was told they never met, for though they were all
Anabaptists, yet for some collateral differences, they
detested one another, and though many of them were
near in blood and alliance to one another, yet the
son would excommunicate the father in the room
above him, and the nephew the uncle. As St. John
is said to have quitted that bath into which Cerinthus
the heretic came, so did I this house. I remember
that Hezekiah in his sickness turned himself in his
bed to pray to that wall that looked to Jerusalem,
and that Daniel in Babylon, when he prayed in his
chamber, opened those windows that looked towards
Jerusalem; for in the first dedication of the temple
at Jerusalem there is a promise annexed to the
prayers made towards the temple, and I began to
think how many roofs, how many floors of separation,
were made between God and my prayers in that
house. And such is this multiplicity of sins which
we consider to be got over us as a roof, as an arch;
many arches, many roofs; for though these habitual
sins be so of kin, as that they grow from one
another, and yet for all this kindred excommunicate
one another (for covetousness will not be in the same

room with prodigality), yet it is but going up another stair, and there is the other Anabaptist; it is but living a few years and then the prodigal becomes covetous. All the way they separate us from God as a roof, as an arch, and then an arch will bear any weight, an habitual sin got over our head as an arch will stand under any sickness, any dishonour, any judgment of God, and never sink towards any humiliation."

It was not long after his appointment to the Readership at Lincoln's Inn that Donne's sermons began to attract notice, and he soon became recognised as a great preacher.

When James I. started on his memorable "Progress" to Scotland on the 15th March 1617, he appears to have ordered that Donne should preach at Paul's Cross on the 24th March, the anniversary of his coming to the crown. There was a great gathering of "the Lords of the Council and other honourable persons," including the Archbishop of Canterbury (Abbot), Lord Bacon (who had been recently made Lord Keeper), the Lord Privy Seal, secretary Winwood, and "divers other great men," including Donne's fast friend, Sir Julius Cæsar, Master of the Rolls, and Lord Hay. It was Donne's first appearance in the famous metropolitan pulpit, and he showed himself worthy of the occasion. One who was present writes that "Dr. Donne made them a dainty sermon upon Proverbs xxii. 11: '*He that loveth pureness of heart, for the grace of his lips the king shall be his friend;*' and was exceedingly liked generally (*i.e.* by all), the rather that he did Queen Elizabeth right, and held himself close to the text without flattering the time too much." "The dainty sermon"

scarcely expresses adequately the real loftiness of
tone and earnestness which characterise it. It must
have taken more than an hour to deliver, for it is
very long. Here is the passage concerning Queen
Elizabeth referred to—a passage which, in that age of
adulation when courtiers were shy of doing honour to
the great queen, must have seemed to many almost
an instance of audacious outspokenness.

"In the death of that queen, unmatchable, inimitable in her sex, we were all under one common flood
and depth of tears . . . Of her we may say, *nihil
humile aut abjectum cogitavit quia novit de se semper
loquendum. She knew the world would talk of her*
after her death, and therefore she did such things all
her life as were worthy to be talked of. Of her
glorious successor and our gracious sovereign we may
say it would have troubled any king but him to
have come in succession and in comparison with such
a queen."

Donne was now a prosperous man; but during this
year, 1617, and less than three years after his ordination, a great sorrow came upon him. His much-loved
wife died on the 15th August, seven days after the
birth of her twelft¹ child. She was in her thirty-
sixth year, Donne in his forty-fourth,—of her children
seven survived her. In the first agony of his grief he
gave his children an assurance that he would never
marry again, and this when his eldest child was only
fourteen and his youngest an infant in arms. The
promise was a rash one. It would perhaps have been
better for him, and better for them, if it had never
been made.   ead, and , ...

Mrs. Donne w¹ president.   ⌐ Danes

Church, where a monument was erected in the chancel
to her memory, with an elaborate inscription which
her husband himself composed. The old church has
been rebuilt, and the monument has long since
perished ; the inscription has been preserved by the
accident that Donne submitted it for approval to Sir
George More, and it is still to be found among the
muniments at Losely.

The story that Donne preached a funeral sermon
upon his wife in St. Clement's Church, upon the text,
Lamentations iii. 1, is a fable. He did preach a
beautiful sermon upon this text some ten years later,
which is to be found among his printed works, but it
is nothing like a funeral sermon, and it was preached
at St. Dunstan's Church, to which he was only in-
stituted in 1623.

During the next two years we find Donne frequently
preaching at Whitehall, besides diligently attending
to his duties at Lincoln's Inn. On the 28th March
1619, being Easter Day, he was called upon to preach
before the Lords at a time of great public anxiety.
Queen Anne of Denmark had died on the first of the
month, and James I., after taking his leave of his
consort, had gone to Newmarket. Here he had himself fallen seriously ill, and on the day when Donne
preached at Whitehall he was reported to be
" dangerously sick." It was not until the middle of
April that the Bishop of London preached at St.
Paul's, to give thanks for the king's recovery.

.   .   .   .   .   .

Just eight days before Donne preached to the
Lords at Whitehall the Emperor Matthias died suddenly the time too much." " The He had become

King of Bohemia, after the enforced resignation of the crown by his incompetent brother, Rudolph II., in May 1611; and on the death of that same brother, eight months later, 20th January 1612, he was elected to succeed him as emperor. Neither of the brothers had any legitimate offspring, and, in view of what might happen after his decease, Matthias so ordered it that his kinsman, the Archduke Ferdinand of Styria, should succeed to the crown of Bohemia, *the States consenting to the arrangement* in June 1617, he himself still retaining the imperial crown.

The Bohemian nobility, a powerful oligarchical body, were vehemently Protestant. Ferdinand, the new king, was an uncompromising and bigoted Catholic. Before a year had passed, Bohemia was in open revolt, the country and its people were suffering the horrors of war when the Emperor Matthias died. The crisis was a very great one. Could nothing be done to make peace between Ferdinand and his Bohemian subjects? A proposal came to James I. that he should act as arbitrator between the belligerents. Nothing loth, the king ordered Lord Hay, now Earl of Doncaster, to proceed to Germany as his Ambassador Extraordinary, with instructions which were of the vaguest kind. "And by special command of His Majesty, Dr. Donne was appointed to assist and attend that employment to the Princes of the Union." [1]

Ostensibly, Donne went as his noble friend's chaplain, and before he set out upon his travels he preached

---

[1] The German Princes at this time were divided by their religious differences into two hostile parties—the Catholic *League*, of which Ferdinand was the head, and the Protestant *Union*, under Frederick the Elector Palatine as president.

what he calls "a sermon of valediction at my going
into Germany," at Lincoln's Inn, on the text, "Remember now thy Creator in the days of thy youth"
(Eccles. xii. 1), in which the preacher closed with the
following beautiful and pathetic exordium :—

"Now to make up a circle, by returning to our first
word, remember: as we remember God, so for His
sake, let us remember one another.   In my long
absence, and far distance from hence, remember me,
as I shall do you . . . remember my labours and
endeavours, at least my desire, to make sure your
salvation.   And I shall remember your religious
cheerfulness in hearing the word, and your christianly
respect towards all them that bring that word unto
you, and towards myself in particular far above my
merit.   And so as your eyes that stay here, and mine
that must be far off, for all that distance shall meet
every morning, in looking upon that same sun, and
meet every night, in looking upon the same moon; so
our hearts may meet morning and evening in that
God, which sees and hears everywhere; that you may
come thither to Him with your prayers, that I (if I
may be of use for His glory, and your edification in this
place) may be restored to you again; and may come
to Him with my prayer, that what Paul soever plant
amongst you, or what Apollos soever water, God Himself will give the increase: that if I never meet you
again till we have all passed the gate of death, yet in
the gates of heaven, I may meet you all, and there say
to my Saviour and your Saviour, that which He said to
His Father and our Father, *Of those whom thou hast
given me, have I not lost one.*   Remember me thus, you
that stay in this kingdom of peace, where no sword is

drawn, but the sword of justice, as I shall remember
you in those kingdoms, where ambition on one side,
and a necessary defence from unjust persecution on
the other side hath drawn many swords; and Christ
Jesus remember us all in His kingdom . . . where we
shall be all soldiers of one army, the Lord of hosts,
and children of one choir, the God of harmony and
consent; where all clients shall retain but one coun-
sellor, our advocate Christ Jesus; . . . where we shall
end, and yet begin but then; where we shall have
continual rest, and yet never grow lazy; where we
shall be stronger to resist, and yet have no enemy;
where we shall live and never die, where we shall
meet and never part."

The sermon was preached on the 18th of April,
and on the 12th May Doncaster and his retinue set
out on their journey, and arrived early in June at
Heidelberg, the palace of the Elector Palatine Frederick and his wife Elizabeth, daughter of James I.
Six years before this these two illustrious personages
had been married at Whitehall, and Donne had written
the marriage song;[1] they were both nearly of the same
age, each being now twenty-two years old. Since
that brilliant wedding-day, in February 1613, their
lives had been passed in one continual round of gaiety
and amusement. The young Palsgrave, as he was
usually called in England, had learned very little:
dreaming of greatness, he had not been preparing
himself to achieve it. A young man of restless ambition far beyond his ability, he was certain to prove a
failure in the day of trial; and that day was very near
at hand. During those six years Donne had greatly

[1] See p. 83.

changed and greatly grown; the young princess may
have remembered him as a courtier high in favour
with the nobility, writing verses to order, graceful and
gay, whom her royal father had pressed to enter into
the Christian ministry, and had obeyed only when all
other avenues to advancement had been barred. She
found him now a profoundly serious and earnest
divine, who already had come to be regarded as one
of the greatest preachers of his time. He had not
been many days at Heidelberg before he was invited
to preach before the Prince and Princess Palatine.

The Princess Elizabeth appears to have been greatly
struck by the sermons (for there were two, though
only one has been preserved), and from this time conceived a high regard for Donne, and, in a letter which
she wrote to him four years later, she says, " The hearing of you deliver, as you call them, the messages of
God unto me . . . truly I never did but with delight,
and I hope some measure of edification."

The stay at Heidelberg was short. Doncaster soon
began to suspect that his mission to Germany was
not likely to be successful. Ferdinand was chosen
emperor on the 18th of August, and had hardly
heard of his election before the amazing intelligence
reached him that, two days before, the Bohemian
magnates had solemnly deposed him from being king,
and had offered his crown to Frederick, the Palsgrave.

Frederick hesitated for about a month before accept-
ing the kingdom. At last he assented, and in October
he set out for Prague for his coronation, which, alas !
was but the beginning of his humiliation, and all the
long horrors of the Thirty Years' War. Doncaster's
wanderings during the next five months are difficult to

follow, but on the 19th December he was at the Hague, where the States General presented Donne with the gold medal that had been struck as a memorial of the famous and futile Synod of Dort, which had recently dispersed.

At the Hague, Donne (apparently with but short warning) was called upon to preach before the Court and the States General that sermon which he expanded into two during his last illness.

Lord Doncaster returned to England with his retinue during the first week of 1620. Donne had derived much benefit from his eight months' absence, and during the spring he preached more than once at Whitehall; his ordinary duties at Lincoln's Inn being resumed as before his absence. We know very little of his movements during this year, 1621, except that in the summer he was disappointed of the Deanery of Salisbury, which had fallen vacant, and which he had expected would be offered to him. He had to wait a little longer before receiving any substantial preferment.

On the 26th of August 1621, Cotton, Bishop of Exeter, died, and a month later Valentine Carey, Dean of St. Paul's, was elected to succeed him.

Then it seems "the king sent to Dr. Donne and appointed him to attend him at dinner the next day. When His Majesty was sat down, before he had eat any meat, he said, after his pleasant manner, 'Dr. Donne, I have invited you to dinner; and, though you sit not down with me, yet I will carve to you of a dish that I know you love well; for, knowing you love London, I do therefore make you Dean of St. Paul's; and, when I have dined, then do you take

9

your beloved dish home to your study, say grace there to yourself, and much good may it do you.' "

He did not actually enter upon his office till the 27th November, as, in consequence of the delay which occurred in the consecration of the Bishop of Exeter, the deanery did not technically fall into the hands of the king till the 20th of the month. There is no reason to believe that Donne expected or wished to be raised to the Episcopate. Probably, he had now gained the one piece of preferment in the Church of England that he would have chosen if the choice had been left to himself. The deanery stood in the south of the present cathedral, with its frontage towards the north, and its back gates opening upon Carter Lane. There was a gatehouse and porter's lodge at either entrance, and a spacious grass-plot on the east side. There was a private chapel annexed to the house and flanking the grass-plot on the southern side; this chapel the new dean at once set himself to repair and beautify. The expense of furnishing and getting into so large a mansion was considerable; and it is not surprising that Donne, at the end of his first year, wrote to his friend Sir Henry Goodere, " I had locked myself, sealed and secured myself, against all possibilities of falling into new debts, and, in good faith, this year hath thrown me £400 lower than when I entered this house." Nevertheless, the very first occasion after receiving his preferment, when Sir George More offered to pay the quarterly sum which he had agreed to allow him, Donne refused to accept it, and then and there gave him a release from the obligation by which he was bound.

CHAPTER VI

THE DEAN

DURING the seven years that passed after Donne had been admitted to holy orders, it cannot be said that he had made much way in his profession. A couple of benefices given to him by personal friends—the Preachership at Lincoln's Inn, and the barren honour of being included among the king's chaplains—did not amount to much. His income during these years was indeed sufficient to relieve him from any pressing anxiety; but, moving as he did on terms of close intimacy with the nobility and the most eminent people of the court of James I., his position brought with it many expenses which were unavoidable.

The deanery had come only after years of waiting for the fulfilment of those hopes of preferment which the king had given his chaplain reason to expect at his hands.

Thus far, it must be remembered, Donne had had few opportunities of addressing large and mixed congregations. Lincoln's Inn Chapel, was then, as now, a place of worship for a select few. At Whitehall the nobility and courtiers made up the whole audience. The sermon at St. Paul's, preached during the king's absence in Scotland, had indeed attracted a great crowd, and had been listened to with admiration by all; but, until his promotion to the deanery, Donne as a preacher may be said to have been little known. Among the general public he had his reputation still to make. He continued to hold the Lincoln's Inn Preachership for some months after he was admitted to the deanery. Not till the 11th of February did he resign his office, and, in doing so, he presented a magnificent copy of the Bible, with the commentary of Nicholas de Lyra, in six volumes folio, printed at Douai in 1617, as a token of gratitude to the society. The book is carefully preserved in Lincoln's Inn library; and the inscription, in Donne's own handwriting, may still be read by those who are not above confessing to a sentimental interest in such relics.

In recognition of this gift and of his services as preacher, we read that " The Masters of the Bench acknowledging this and many other kind and loving respects of the said Mr. Doctor Donne towards them . . . with one voice and assent so ordered that the said Mr. Doctor Donne shall continue his chamber in this house which he now hath, *as a Bencher of this house*, and with such privileges touching the same as the Masters of the Bench now have, and ought to have, for their general and respective chambers in this house."

It may, I think, be safely affirmed that this is the last instance of a divine having been made a Bencher of Lincoln's Inn, and that, too, not only with an honorary title, but with the substantial advantages which the office confers.

.   .   .   .   .   .

Then, as now, the Chapter of St. Paul's consisted of thirty prebendaries, of whom the dean was one, and

each of them had certain prescribed duties to perform.
Among the prebendaries were more than one man of
academic reputation with a career before him. Such
were John Bancroft, afterwards Bishop of Oxford, and
William Pierse, promoted to the Bishopric of Peter-
borough the year before Donne died; Dr. Thomas
Winniffe, who succeeded Donne in the deanery, and
afterwards became Bishop of Lincoln; and the brothers
John and Henry King, sons of John King, Bishop of
London, who had been chaplain to the Lord Keeper
Ellesmere when Donne had been his secretary. The
only two members of the Chapter, nevertheless, who
appear to have had any gift of preaching, were Dr.
Winniffe and Henry Mason, rector of St. Mary's Under-
shaft London, of whose "edifying and judicious preaching" Wood speaks in high terms. He had been chaplain
to Bishop King of London, by whom, too, he had been
collated to his stall. The bishop's two sons had been
presented to their several prebends by their father in
1616—Henry, the elder, in January; John, the younger,
in December; the one in his twenty-fourth, the other
in his twenty-second year. They were both young
men of conspicuous ability. Henry was a poet, whose
sweet verses are read with delight by many even now,
—a man of letters and many accomplishments. John
was a young scholar of promise, who became public
orator to the University of Oxford at the time that
George Herbert held the same honourable office at
Cambridge; Donne had known them both from their
childhood. The younger brother was little heard of
in London; he was a brilliant scholar, and his heart
was at Oxford. The elder, Henry, besides being prebendary at St. Paul's, was collated by his father to

the Archdeaconry of Colchester in 1617; and with
the Rectory of Chigwell he also held the office of
Penitentiary in the cathedral. His preferments required that he should reside during the greater part
of the year in London, and Walton calls him the
" Chief Residentiary of St. Paul's." Donne appears
always to have had an affectionate regard for Henry
King—an affection which was cordially reciprocated
by the younger man; and in his will Donne appointed
him one of his executors, as we shall see later on. As
for Dr. Valentine Cary, who had vacated the Deanery
of St. Paul's for the Bishopric of Exeter, he had the
reputation of being a past master in the art of
"getting on." An eminently safe man, he had never
committed himself to the writing of books, and as a
preacher of sermons he was unknown. It is true that
the famous pulpit at Paul's Cross still continued to be
served occasionally by ambitious, earnest, and eloquent
preachers from the country—men eager to get a hearing and make a sensation before a London audience;
but the ordinary sermons delivered in rotation by the
prebendaries taking their turns in the cathedral pulpit
must have been, as a rule, very perfunctory perform-
ances. The preachers who had the ear of the London
citizens were by no means the cathedral dignitaries,
but the men of a lower social standing, though not
necessarily of less learning or less worth listening to,
the lecturers whose congregations supported them,—
the holders of small benefices which barely afforded
them a livelihood,—the Puritans, as they were called,
which was a term of reproach vaguely applied to such
as were conspicuous less for strict orthodoxy than for
fervour, fluency, and passionate eloquence. As a class,·

these clergy were not too loyal to the ecclesiastical *status quo*. They had very little to thank, and very little to hope from, the powers that be in Church and State. Some of them were more zealous than discreet, more vehement than prudent, and the neglect which they suffered at the hands of "people of importance" often irritated and soured their friends and admirers perhaps more than it did themselves. In so far as it did so, however, their influence undoubtedly tended to make a party of opposition in the Church, which sooner or later was likely to become a formidable minority, and indeed something more.

Archbishop Abbot's sympathies were almost wholly in favour of the Puritan clergy, and in the universities they had their leaders and representatives, who were increasing in numbers from year to year.

There can be no greater mistake than to look upon the Puritan clergy as schismatics; they were no more inclined that way than John Wesley was in the last century, or than the Low Church party, who loved to preach in the black gown, or the Tractarians, who battled for the eastward position in our own day, were, or are, inclined to separate from our communion. Intolerant partisans on this side or the other invented some odious name for such as were not of their own way of thinking; and it has always answered the purpose of such as are fighting for no nobler cause than the supremacy of their own views, in politics or religion, to call their opponents Simeonites or Puseyites in the one case, and Whigs or Tories in the other. Would God that the spirit of faction could have been kept out of the Church of Christ! Alas! .from the very beginning it has shown itself, ever since one said, I am of Paul, and another, I am of Apollos!

The new Dean of St. Paul's was as far from sympathising with this narrowness as in those days a man could well be. He had by God's help found deliverance from the thraldom of the Roman tyranny as formulated in the Tridentine decrees, but he was not the man to oscillate from extreme to extreme, and to find no resting-place save in one or the other. He had his spiritual conflicts, and he had passed through an experience such as shallow natures can hardly be expected to understand. He could never rest till he got to some firm basis of belief, before he adopted any opinion as his own; he had a boundless sympathy for the errors and the weaknesses of others; he had the rare gift of living by great principles, not by mere hard-and-fast rules, the poet's wealth of illustration and play of fancy, and the voice and readiness of speech of the orator. Add to this the extraordinary personal beauty and resistless grace of manner which more than one of his contemporaries have dwelt upon. "A preacher in earnest," as Walton says, "weeping sometimes for his auditory, sometimes with them; always preaching to himself, like an angel from a cloud, but in none; carrying some, as St. Paul was, to heaven in holy raptures, and enticing others by a sacred art and courtship to amend their lives; here picturing a vice so as to make it ugly to those that practised it; and a virtue so as to make it beloved, even by those that loved it not; and all this with a most particular grace and an inexpressible addition of comeliness."

Donne's five years' preaching at Lincoln's Inn had

done a great deal for him in the way of increasing his effectiveness as a pulpit orator. The reading of sermons was scarcely tolerated at this time; even in the university pulpit, where the practice was coming in, James I. had written a letter expressing his disapproval of it. In Donne's time, our English preachers, on great occasions, almost universally committed their sermons to memory, as is still done in Italy, Germany, France, and elsewhere. When a man ascended the pulpit, he "took with him words"; he was not supposed to be speaking without due preparation; but the habit of addressing his congregation without a manuscript gave a preacher confidence on the one hand, and on the other made him realise the necessity of careful previous study of his subject. The memory was cultivated from the first. Fluency with the graces of distinct delivery were not disregarded; and only he who really gave proof of having something to say, and of having tried to say it in the most attractive manner, was designated as a *painful* preacher, that is, one who had spent his best pains upon matter and manner.

This severe and systematic training on pulpit oratory, which English preachers went through in the earlier half of the seventeenth century, necessarily produced its effect in raising the standard of preaching. The sermons of this time seem to us now to be overloaded—too long—artificial, and sometimes in bad taste; but it is rare to find one without some striking passages, some evidence or parade of learning. That they were listened to with great attention, and often produced very great effect upon the audience, we know. Frequently the preacher was interrupted

by expressions of dissent or by loud applause. More
than once Donne takes notice of this, reproving it as
a modern practice which had but lately come into
vogue, though, as he points out, it had been common
in the fourth century, when Chrysostom preached at
Constantinople, and Augustine at Hippo.

"Truly," he says in one of his St. Paul's sermons,
" we come too near reinducing this vainglorious fashion,
in those often periodical murmurings and noises
which you make when the preacher concludes any
point. For those impertinent interjections swallow
up one quarter of his hour; and many that were not
within distance of hearing the sermon will give a
censure upon it, according to the frequency or paucity
of these acclamations.

" These fashions then, howsoever, in those times,
they might be testimonies of zeal, yet because they
occasion vainglory and many times faction, . . .
we desire not, willingly we admit not. We come in
Christ's stead. Christ, at His coming, met *Hosannas*
and *Crucifiges*. A preacher may be applauded in the
pulpit and crucified in his turn."

It is very unlikely that the congregation in Lincoln's
Inn Chapel, accustomed as they were to the seriousness and strict discipline of the law courts, should
have indulged in these expressions of approval or the
reverse; on the other hand, the men of law were
severe critics, and a great deal was expected from
their preacher. During the five years when Donne
held the post he was responsible for an aggregate
of between two or three hundred sermons, and every
one of them stood for such an amount of careful
preparation as represented a serious mental strain.

But that all these sermons should have been written out word for word and committed to memory is incredible; it would have been almost a physical impossibility. In one of his letters Donne mentions incidentally that the copying of one of his great festival sermons took him eight hours; and we know that he was compelled, by the importunity of his friends, to circulate some of them in manuscript before he ventured to incur the expense of printing them. Once, when replying to a request from Sir Henry Goodere to send him a copy of what appears to have been an occasional sermon, which he had delivered some weeks before, he answers, "I will pretermit no time to write it . . . though in good faith *I have half forgot it.*" Of all the large number of sermons delivered at Lincoln's Inn, only fourteen have come down to us. It is clear that before he was promoted to the deanery he must have become a practised extempore preacher. It was only what was to be expected, that when he discovered that he possessed the gift of oratory, and had done his best to cultivate it earnestly and conscientiously, he should come to take a delight in its exercise; though for lazy and slovenly preaching he had no toleration, and more than once he lifts up his voice against the preachers who trusted to the so-called inspiration of the moment.

"When the apostle says, *Study to be quiet*, methinks he intimates something towards *this*—that the less we study for our sermons, the more danger there is to disquiet the auditory. Extemporal, unpremeditated sermons, that serve the popular ear, vent, for the most part, doctrines that disquiet the Church. Study for

them, and they will be quiet. Consider ancient
fundamental doctrine, and this will quiet and settle
the understanding and the conscience."

For himself, every year as he grew older, he seems
to have found more and more joy and delight in
preaching. Latterly, even when his constitution was
broken by frequent illnesses and the excitement and
exhaustion which his emphatic delivery occasioned, he
confesses to his friend, Sir Robert Carr, that his
practice was to fast rigidly on his preaching days.

"This morning I have received a signification from
my Lord Chamberlain that His Majesty hath commanded to-morrow's sermon at St. James's; and that
it is in the afternoon—for, into my mouth there must
not enter the word 'after dinner,' because that day
there enters no dinner into my mouth. Towards the
time of the service, I ask your leave that I may hide
myself in your out-chamber." (2nd April 1625.)

In another letter, again, he writes, ". . . I do not
eat before, *nor can after*, till I have been at home; so
much hath this year's debility disabled me even for
receiving favours. After the sermon I will steal into
my coach home, and pray that my good purpose may
be well accepted, and my defects graciously pardoned."

Five years later, when already death-stricken, and
very near his end, writing to another of those many
friends who had clung to him in close intimacy from
his youth, he says, ". . . I have been always more
sorry when I could not preach, than any could be that
they could not hear me. It hath been my desire—and
God may be pleased to grant it me—that I might die
in the pulpit; if not that, yet that I might take my
death in the pulpit, that is, die the sooner by occasion

of my former labours." It can hardly be doubted that
he hastened his end by preaching when he was physi-
cally quite unfit for such exertion; but life was, to
his thinking, valueless when the privilege of delivering
his Master's message to sinful men was denied him.
And so, as Walton beautifully says, "his speech, which
had long been his ready and faithful servant, left him
not till the last minute of his life, and then forsook
him, not to serve another master—for who speaks
like him?—but died before him; for that it was then
become useless to him that now conversed with God
on earth, as angels are said to do in heaven, only by
thoughts and looks."

.   .   .   .   .   .

The duties required of the Dean of St. Paul's were
definitely prescribed by the cathedral statutes.

The Psalter was divided up among the thirty prebendaries, each of whom was supposed to recite
his five psalms daily, and to make them his special
subject of meditation. Donne took his place in the
Chapter as prebendary of Chiswick, and his five psalms
were the 62nd to the 66th inclusive. As prebendary
he was required to preach upon the Monday in Whit-
sun week. As dean he preached on Christmas Day,
Easter Sunday, and Whit Sunday. Every one of the
Easter sermons have been preserved, and are to be
found in the printed volumes; so are all those which
he delivered on Whit Sunday. Twice, owing to severe
illness, he was unable to preach on Christmas Day; but
the eight Christmas sermons that he did deliver at St.
Paul's are among the most carefully thought out and
most eloquent of any that have survived.

The same may be said of the five prebend sermons

delivered on his allotted psalms. On the great festivals he did not spare himself; and on these important occasions, when large congregations came expecting much from the great preacher, he never sent them empty away.

His first appearance in the pulpit of St. Paul's as dean was on Christmas Day 1621. The sermon is unlike any of those which he had preached at Lincoln's Inn or at the court. It is marked by an almost entire absence of learned quotations or allusions. It is studiously direct, practical, and homely; and though the structure and *analysis* of the composition is as minute as he could not help making it, this sermon is marked by such simplicity of diction and illustration as makes it apparent that the preacher was thinking of his congregation and not of himself, seeking to reach their hearts and consciences, with never a thought of merely winning their admiration and applause.

Though no word has reached us of the reception which Donne met with on his first appearance as dean, yet there are abundant indications that his first sermon made a great impression. Certainly, in no one year was he applied to so frequently to address large audiences as in 1622.

No fewer than twelve of his most important sermons, delivered during this year, have been preserved. Unequal in merit, they are yet all characterised by an almost excessive elaboration, as if the new dean was profoundly convinced of the responsibility which his office had brought with it, and was determined, by God's help, to turn to the utmost account the influence which he had the opportunities of exercising.

As a theologian, Donne occupied a middle position between the two extreme parties among the clergy, whose differences were becoming daily more pronounced, and their attitude more hostile towards each other. On the burning questions of the ceremonies and the sacraments, he was emphatically a High Churchman, outspoken, uncompromising, definite, though gentle, sympathetic, and animated by a large-hearted tolerance. But in his treatment of Holy Scriptures no Puritan of them all insisted more frequently upon the inspiration of every syllable in the Old Testament and the New. With far less of that trifling with his hearers, which is too frequently the blemish in Bishop Andrewes' sermons, Donne's interpretations occasionally startle us by their grotesqueness; they are the outcome of his almost superstitious *bibliolatry*, if this modern phrase may be allowed. It was this, however, which gained for him the ear of the trading classes, and the confidence and popularity which never left him. Both parties in the Church claimed him as their own. Abbot, the Puritan primate, trusted and admired him; Andrewes loved him as a friend; Laud would have recognised him, with some reservations, as one of his most orthodox supporters. It was this many-sidedness that attracted the thoughtful and devout to listen to the message he came to deliver. He spoke like one who had studied and prayed out the conclusions he arrived at; men felt they could leave themselves in the hands of the new preacher, who was no partisan. Three of Donne's sermons during this year, 1622, preached on occasions of some historical interest, deserve rather more than a passing mention.

1. In the summer of 1621, Henry Percy, ninth

Earl of Northumberland (who, it may be remembered,[1]
had gone out of his way to intercede with Sir George
More on the occasion of Donne's clandestine marriage),
was released from the Tower, after an imprisonment
of nearly sixteen years, through the intercession of
Donne's friend, Lord Hay, now Viscount Doncaster.
Doncaster had married the earl's beautiful and very
accomplished daughter Lucy, without her father's
consent, and during the time of his imprisonment.
The king had favoured the match. The earl was
strongly averse to it, and hated Doncaster, whom he
affected to regard as a Scotch upstart. Northumberland, though freed from the Tower, was put upon
parole, and required to reside at Petworth, or within
thirty miles of that centre. It was an annoying
restriction, and Doncaster did his best to get it
removed. On his return from an embassy to France
in 1622, he made fresh efforts to gain full liberty
for the earl, who about the middle of August found
himself a free man. But he had not yet forgiven his
son-in-law; and, moreover, he had conceived a bitter dis-
like for the king's new favourite, Villiers, now Marquis
of Buckingham, whose ostentation and lavish expenditure provoked and irritated him. He regarded
himself, as indeed he was, as the representative of
the old nobility, and he found it very difficult to
acquiesce in the position (which common prudence
required that he should submit to) of inferior importance to the new men, who on all occasions were
taking the lead at court. So wary and shrewd a
diplomatist as Doncaster saw that this attitude was
full of danger. He himself was at this time living

[1] Chap. i. p. 23.

at Hanworth, which had formerly been the dower house of Queen Katharine Parr, and here Lady Doncaster was keeping up a great establishment, and indulging in every kind of profuse extravagance. Some recognition of his son-in-law's good offices in procuring him his release from the Tower could hardly be refused now, and Northumberland accepted an invitation to Hanworth on the 25th of August, knowing, of course, that in doing so he would be signifying his assent to the marriage which he had originally opposed. It was a great occasion. Many of the nobility were assembled to show their sympathy with the earl, and their satisfaction at his once more taking his place as head of the English aristocracy. Among them came Buckingham himself, ready to evince his cordiality, and having nothing to lose, and something to gain, by taking part in the festivities. On such an occasion it was inevitable that there should be a sermon, and what fitter man could be thought of to preach it than the new Dean of St. Paul's ?

About a year before this, Donne, at the suggestion of the king,[1] had offered his services to Villiers; but, so far as we know, nothing had come of it, except that his name was formally presented to James as a proper person to be promoted to the deanery.

Donne's sermon at Hanworth was preached from a text that might almost be called fantastic. "Every man may see it; man may behold it afar off" (Job xxxvi. 25). After a brief introductory paragraph the preacher comes to his analysis. "Be pleased to admit, and charge your memories with this distribution of the words. . . . I threaten you but with two parts,

[1] *Cabala*, p. 314.

10

no further tediousness, but I ask for divers branches.
I can promise no more shortness. . . . The first is a
discovery, a manifestation of God to man. *Every man
may see it.* . . . This proposition, this discovery, will
be the first part, and the other will be a tacit answer
to a likely objection : 'Is not God far off, and can
man see at that distance?' Yes! he may. *Man
may behold it afar off.*"

The sermon is one of the shortest of Donne's
sermons, and ends so abruptly as to leave the impression that it never was delivered exactly in the
form in which it has come down to us. I think it is
an instance of Donne's having written out his recollec-
tions of what he actually said, assisted by notes which
he had prepared. There are some delicate allusions to
the vicissitudes of fortune through which the Earl of
Northumberland had passed, which everyone present
must have understood. But the concluding passage
loses none of its point, because the personal allusions
are so gracefully veiled under the disguise of
generalities in the language.

The festivities at Hanworth brought Donne into more
intimate relations with Buckingham, and the result was
that a few weeks later he was called upon by the king
to discharge a duty of much delicacy and difficulty.

2. This was to preach a sermon at St. Paul's, which
should be a defence of His Majesty's *Instructions to
Preachers* recently issued by authority, and which had
proved by no means acceptable to a large section of
the clergy and their congregations.

For some years before this a movement had been
going on at Oxford, which was slowly effecting a
reaction against the hitherto dominant Calvinism of

the Puritan clergy. The consecration of Laud to the
Bishopric of St. Asaph, on the 18th November 1621,
had been regarded as a great encouragement to his
friends, but it had provoked into most unseemly
language many of the more violent of his opponents.
There was great excitement up and down the country,
and the preachers hurled defiance against those with
whom they were at variance. James I., as usual,
believing that he could settle anything by issuing a
proclamation or an order, put forth certain " instructions " to the preachers, which read as if the king
intended to restrict the liberty of speech hitherto
allowed to the pulpit, and seemed to foreshadow the
silencing of one of the two Church parties by the
other in the near future. As mere advice, no
exception could be taken to the words of these
instructions, " but, coming as they did, as an attempt
to enforce silence on the great questions of the day,
they only served to embitter the quarrel which they
were meant to calm." [1]

As might have been expected, the popular excitement increased ; and the king, thinking to allay it
among the Londoners by appointing so popular a
preacher as the new dean to explain the meaning and
intention of the *Instructions*, ordered Donne to preach
at St. Paul's Cross on the 14th September, and act as
his spokesman and interpreter to the people. There
was an immense crowd,—" as large a congregation as
I ever saw," writes Donne,—but the effect of the
sermon appears to have been not at all as great as
was looked for. Indeed, it is but a poor specimen of

[1] S. R. Gardiner, *Prince Charles and the Spanish Marriage*, ch. x.
p. 233.

pulpit oratory; it is an apology carefully drawn up, but cold and passionless. There is, however, one curious passage which deserves quoting, as illustrative of the habits of the Londoners at this time, and of their passion for the study of Holy Scripture, which extended even to the working-classes. Speaking of the great necessity there was for the people to be taught the Catechism, and to be instructed in the elements of Christian doctrine, Donne says, "If you should tell some men that Calvin's Institution were a catechism, would they not love catechising the better for that name?"

The sermon was immediately published "by commandment of His Majesty," with an epistle dedicatory addressed to Villiers, now High Admiral and Marquis of Buckingham. I do not think it met with any large sale, and there is no sign that a second edition was ever called for.

3. A very different sermon was that which Donne preached two months later before the Virginia Company, in which he himself was an adventurer, or shareholder, and indeed was one of the council.

This sermon may, with truth, be called the first *missionary sermon* ever preached in England since Britain had become a Christian land. The Virginia Company had been started in 1610 by a large number of the nobility, gentry, London merchants, and clergy, partly as a commercial and partly as a philanthropical and missionary undertaking on a very ambitious scale. It had proved, during its first ten years, an unsuccessful speculation, and its affairs had been grossly mismanaged. About 1620, things had come to such a pass that the Company were divided into two parties, who were quarrelling violently; and when the saintly Nicholas Ferrar, as executor to his father, was called on to administer to the old merchant's estate, he appears to have found it necessary to look very closely into the accounts of the Company, of which the elder Mr. Ferrar had been one of the founders and a large shareholder.

The history of the Virginia Company has not yet been written, and the materials for writing that history have only recently been made available for research. It looks, however, as if Nicholas Ferrar and his enthusiastic friends were trying to bring the religious and missionary element into far greater prominence than had been done even from the beginning; and it is not unlikely that the hope of utilising the resources of the Company, for bringing about the conversion of the Indians to Christianity, was the strong motive which urged Nicholas Ferrar to take so active a part in the attempt to put the finances upon a safe basis. In 1622 Lord Southampton, Shakespeare's early friend and patron, was chosen treasurer, and Nicholas Ferrar deputy. It must have been at their invitation that Donne was invited to preach before the Company, and to impress upon the *adventurers*, who included among them a large number of bishops, clergy, and devout laity, an appeal from the missionary point of view which would be likely to produce a great effect. Unfortunately, some months earlier, the dreadful tidings had arrived that the Indians in the colony had risen and massacred some six hundred of the settlers, and since then the outlook had not been very reassuring. The occasion did not seem favourable for advocating the duty of proselytising,

yet Donne kept to his point with consummate skill,
and pleaded his cause with a lofty earnestness and
eloquence [1] such as even he has seldom surpassed.
Some of those he addresses were seeking, he says,
" to establish such a government as should not depend
upon this."   Some "propose to themselves an ex-
emption from laws—to live at liberty; some present
benefit and profit, a sudden way to be rich, and an
abundance of all desirable commodities from thence.
. . . All these are not yet in the right way.   O if
you could once bring a catechism to be as good ware
amongst them as a bugle, as a knife, as a hatchet; O
if you would be as ready to hearken at the return of
a ship how many Indians were converted to Christ
Jesus, as what trees, or drugs, or dyes that ship
brought, then you were in your right way, and not
till then; liberty and abundance are characteristic of
kingdoms, and a kingdom is excluded in the text; the
apostles were not to look for it in their employment,
nor you in this plantation." . . .

    " Beloved," he adds, " use godly means, and give God
His leisure.   You cannot sow your corn to-day, and say
it shall be above ground to-morrow. . . . All that you
would have by this plantation, you shall not have; God
binds not Himself to measures.   All that you shall have,
you have not yet; God binds not Himself to times.   But
something you shall have.   Nay! you have already
some great things. . . . The gospel must be preached
to those men to whom ye send. . . . Preach to them
doctrinally.   Preach to them practically.   Examine
them with your justice (as far as consists with your
security), your civility; but influence them with your

---

[1] The text of the sermon was Acts i. 8.

godliness and your religion. . . . Those amongst you
that are old now shall pass out of this world with this
great comfort, that you contributed to the beginning of
that commonwealth and that Church, though they live
not to see the growth thereof to perfection. And you
that are young now, may live to see the enemy as
much impeached by that place, and your friends—yea
children—as well accommodated in that place as any
other. You shall have made this island, which is but
as the suburbs of the old world, a bridge, a gallery to
the new, to join all to that world that shall never grow
old—the kingdom of heaven, and add names to the
books of our chronicles, and to the Book of Life."
  The sermon was immediately published. It had a
very large sale, and contributed greatly to increase
Donne's popularity.
  Early in the year another piece of preferment had
fallen to him—the valuable rectory of Blunham in
Bedfordshire, which had been promised him some years
previously by Charles Grey, Earl of Kent. He held
this living with his deanery till his death, and occasionally went down there, but never appears to have
resided for more than a few weeks at a time. When
the year 1622 came to an end, Donne must have been
in the enjoyment of a considerable income, and he was
freed from all anxieties about providing for his family.
His eldest son, John, had just passed out of Westminster School and been elected to a studentship at
Christ Church, Oxford, and the hand of his daughter
Constance had already been sought in marriage,
though the match did not come off. He himself
never seems to have wished for any higher Church
preferment than that which he enjoyed; but there

must have been many who expected that he would
be moved to the Episcopate. Happily, he died Dean
of St. Paul's: if he had gone up higher we should
hardly have known him as we do, as the greatest
preacher of his time.

CHAPTER VII

DONNE AT ST. DUNSTAN'S

THE year 1623 is a somewhat memorable one in our annals. On the 19th of February Prince Charles, accompanied by Buckingham, and with no more than three attendants, crossed the Channel on the famous journey to Spain, to bring back, if it might be so, the Infanta Maria, sister of Philip IV., as the prince's bride and the future Queen of England. It was a mad adventure; but it had its very serious aspects. The Infanta was the granddaughter of Philip II., consort of our own Queen Mary, who, in the firm belief of the people of England, had been the chief instigator of the execrated Marian persecutions. The Infanta was a devout, even a bigoted member of the Roman communion; and that such a princess should become the wife of the heir to the English throne, and mother of his children, was a dreadful and hateful thought to the great bulk of the nation. The news that the Prince of Wales had actually slipped away and put himself into the power of those whom the Puritan zealots unhesitatingly believed to be capable of any treachery, created an outburst of alarm and dismay such as had not been known since the days of the Armada. Nor was the widespread feeling of anxiety groundless.

Though James I. was only in his fifty-seventh year,

he had been for some time in bad health, and was
frequently ailing. Parliament had been dissolved for
more than a year, and the king had let it be known
that he would not again summon the great council of
the nation. The Archbishop of Canterbury (Abbot)
was in disgrace, and, when consulted, took up a
position of antagonism to the Spanish marriage. The
religious dissensions among the clergy and their
several adherents were acute and increasing in
acrimony. Trade and commerce indeed were flourish-
ing, but there was deep discontent among the rising
middle classes, who were sullenly chafing under
grievances, which they were determined should be
redressed some day ; and while these elements of
discord were fermenting below the surface, James I.,
grown more and more indolent, undecided, and pro-
crastinating as he had grown older, was left in a
position of strange isolation. His consort, Queen
Anne, had been dead just four years (2nd March 1619).
Of the seven children she had borne him only two
survived her. Prince Charles had just put himself
in the power of the hated Spaniards, and his sister,
the so-called Queen of Bohemia, was living with her
children in banishment. There was no one in Britain
nearer by blood to the king than his distant cousin,
Ludovic Stuart, Duke of Lennox, in the peerage of
Scotland.[1] As to who had the best title to the
crown, next in succession to the king's grandchildren,
no one seemed to know, and certainly no one was
audacious enough to assert his claim. The king

[1] He was created Duke of Richmond, in the peerage of England,
17th May 1622, possibly to assure him precedence over any others of
the nobility who claimed to be of the blood royal.

stood alone. Of such festivities and amusements as
had been continual in former years we hear almost
nothing. Over the court a gloom was hanging. Only
twice do we hear of Donne being called upon during this
year to preach any special sermons, viz., on the 25th
April, when the new chapel of Lincoln's Inn (of
which he had himself laid the foundation stone five
years before) was consecrated; and on the 23rd of
October, when a great feast was held in the Temple,
on occasion of fifteen sergeants being admitted to the
degree of the Coif. The sermon was delivered at St.
Paul's in the evening. It came at the end of a very
long day. The rain was falling in torrents—the new
sergeants and their friends "went dabbling on foot
and bareheaded," and how the congregation listened
to the preacher we are not told. But the great
"Sergeants' Feast" was nearly fatal to Donne himself: shortly afterwards he was struck down by a
very serious illness, which appears to have been of a
typhoid character, and for some weeks he was in such
great danger that little hope was entertained of his
recovery. The king sent his own physician to consult
with others on his case, but it was not till the 20th
December that hopes began to be entertained of his
recovery. During all these six or eight weeks of
very serious illness, when he was hovering between
life and death, Donne seems to have kept a kind of
diary, in which he wrote down thoughts that suggested
themselves to him from day to day. He was still
confined to his sickroom when he employed himself
in revising these meditations. Reading was forbidden him by his physicians, though they did not
order him to cease from writing, judging it prudent to

allow him this one indulgence, perhaps because his wonderfully active intellect could not safely be left without some opportunity of exercising itself. Hereupon he determined to prepare for the press that unique volume, which he entitled *Devotions upon Emergent Occasions, and Several Steps in my Sickness.* The following letter to Sir Robert Carr shows that the first issue was printed privately for distribution among his friends. It was dedicated to Prince Charles, and was sent out very early in 1624:—

"Though I have left my bed, I have not left my bedside. I sit there still, and as a prisoner discharged sits at the prison door, to beg fees, so sit I here to gather crumbs. I have used this leisure to put the meditations, had in my sickness, into some such order as may minister some holy delight. They arise to so many sheets (perchance twenty) as that, without staying for that furniture of an epistle that my friends importuned me to print them, I importune my friends to receive them printed. That, being in hand, through this long trunk, that reaches from St. Paul's to St. James's, I whisper into your ear this question, whether there be any uncomeliness or unseasonableness in presenting matter of devotion or mortification to that prince, whom I pray God nothing may ever mortify, but holiness. If you allow my purposes in general, I pray cast your eye upon the title and the epistle, and rectify me in them: I submit substance and circumstance to you, and the poor author of both.

"Your very humble and very thankful servant in Christ Jesus,

"J. DONNE."

Of this first edition I have never seen a copy, but so great was the demand for the book that it became necessary to publish a second edition almost immediately after the first; a third edition was called for in 1626, and others followed. The *Devotions* were printed in a little 12mo volume of 589 pages. Donne, in a letter to a friend whose name has not come down to us, gives the following characteristic account of the method and plan of the work :—

" MY LORD,—To make myself ·believe that our life is something, I use in my thoughts to compare it to something, if it be like anything that is something. It is like a sentence, so much as may be uttered in a breathing, and such a .difference as is in styles is in our lives contracted and dilated. And as in some styles there are open parentheses, sentences within sentences, so there are lives within our lives. I am in such a parenthesis now (in a convalesence), when I thought myself very near my period. God brought me into a low valley, and from thence showed me a high Jerusalem, upon so high a hill as that He thought it fit to bid me stay and gather more breath. This I do by meditating, by expostulating, by praying, for since I am barred of my ordinary diet, which is reading, I make these my exercises, which is another part of physic. And these meditations and expostulations and prayers I am bold to send to your lordship, that, as this which I live now is a kind of a second life, I may deliver myself over to your lordship in this life with the same affection and devotion as made me yours in all my former life, and as long as any image of this world sticks in my soul, shall ever remain in your lordship's," etc.

I have called Donne's *Devotions* a unique work, for it is unique in the circumstances under which it was composed, and not less so in the matter and style of the composition itself. It is difficult to understand how it should ever have been as popular as it undoubtedly was, and it is hardly less difficult to explain how it has continued to exercise a strong fascination over men of very various orders of mind—men of fastidious taste, who might have been expected to be offended by the ruggedness of the style, and men of deeply devout temperament, who, one would have thought, would be shocked by what I can only call the religious familiarity which sometimes approaches to a grotesque profaneness of language.

There is, indeed, a certain interest in following the daily course of the patient's illness and its treatment by the physicians, from what Donne calls "the first grudging of my sickness till the recovery had been assured," and they had taken their leave of him with a warning "of the fearful danger of relapsing." That he should have lived through the severity of the attack and the drastic treatment prescribed is wonderful, but that during all that time of dangerous illness he should have continued to take notes and write them down, and that when he had only just been allowed to sit up in his bed those notes should have been in such a form as allowed of their being prepared for the press, is more wonderful still.

For every day there is (1) a meditation *about* God and His dealings with His servant ; (2) an expostulation *with* God—a kind of protest as if he would know why his Heavenly Father was thus dealing with him ; and (3) a prayer *to* God—a supreme offering of submission and aspiration, of adoring hope and trust and love. But all these outpourings are, in some strange way, at least as much the outpourings of the sanctified intellect as of the heart, and they are expressed in language often hard to follow. The thoughts are packed and crowded into sentences sometimes so confused and entangled that they seem to be stagger-ing under the weight they have to carry ; or, to change the metaphor, it is as if some craftsmen were weaving a hundred threads at once, some fine as gossamer, some coarse as vulgarest tow, till the roughness of the texture almost concealed the pattern on the cloth. We are apt to be irritated by the continual demand upon our close attention, and are impatient of the occasional obscurity, but Donne's contemporaries cared less for a transparent style than for the thoughts that the language was meant to express, and which some-times was half concealed by verbiage. That which did appeal to his contemporaries in the *Devotions* was the intense reality of absorbing and entire trust in the nearness of God, which the book exhibits in every page. Donne " throws himself on God, and unperplext " speaks to Him as a man might to his dearest friend, who knew all his secrets, and loved him with a divine love that would spare him all reproaches. Hence there is no morbid dwelling on sins in the past long since forgiven ; no details of self-accusation in the presence of the Holy One, who is of purer eyes than to behold iniquity ; only a brave confidence in the Father of Mercies, whose gracious Spirit had wrought

a great work in His servant's heart, and would not
leave him even to the end. And all this is what
makes this book to many, even now, a stay and support
in hours when the devotional instinct in the hunger of
the soul calls for strong meat, and not mere milk for
babes.

Extracts or quotations from the *Devotions* will leave
a very inadequate impression upon the reader of the
scope and tone of the work, but the following prayer,
which represents the patient's attitude of supplication
on the fifth day, when "the physician comes," may
serve as a specimen of these pleadings with God:—

"O eternal and most gracious Lord, who calledst
down fire from heaven upon the sinful cities, but *once*,
and openedst the earth to swallow the murmurers,
but *once*, and threwest down the Tower of Siloe upon
sinners, but *once*, but for Thy works of mercy repeatest
them often, and still workest by Thine own patterns,
as Thou broughtest man into this world, by giving
him a helper fit for him here, so whether it be Thy
will to continue me long thus, or to dismiss me by
death, be pleased to afford me the helps fit for both
conditions, either for my weak stay here or my final
transmigration from hence. And if Thou mayest
receive glory by that way (and by all ways, Thou
mayest receive glory), glorify Thyself in preserving
this body from such infections as might withhold
those who would come, or endanger them who do
come, and preserve this soul in the faculties thereof
from all such distempers, as might shake the assurance which myself and others have had, that because
Thou hast loved me, Thou wouldst love me to my
end and at my end. Open none of my doors, not of

my heart, not of mine ears, not of my house, to any
supplanter that would enter to undermine me in my
religion to Thee in the time of my weakness, or to
defame me and magnify himself with false rumours
of such a victory, and surprisal of me after I am
dead. Be my salvation, and plead my salvation:
work it and declare it, and as Thy triumphant shall
be, so let the militant Church be assured that Thou
wast my God, and I Thy servant, to, and in my
consummation. Bless Thou the learning and the
labour of this man, whom Thou sendest to assist me;
and since Thou takest me by the hand and puttest
me into his hands (for I come to him in Thy name,
who in Thy name comes to me), since I clog not my
hopes in him, no, nor my prayers to Thee, with any
limited conditions, but enwrap all in those two
petitions, Thy kingdom come, Thy will be done,
prosper him, and relieve me in Thy way, in Thy time,
and in Thy measure. Amen."

While Donne was still lying in great peril of his
life, his daughter Constance was married to Edward
Allen, the founder of Dulwich College, the bride
being in her twentieth, her husband in his fifty-eighth
year, i.e. seven years older than her father. The
marriage had been arranged some two months before,
and was celebrated at Camberwell on the 3rd
December 1623, from the house of her uncle, Sir
Thomas Grymes, who, as has been mentioned, had
married Margaret, second daughter of Sir George
More of Losely. Parliament assembled on the
18th February 1624, and Convocation was, as a
matter of course, called together at the same time.
Donne was appointed Prolocutor of the Lower House,

11

much against his own wishes. In his opening address to the House, he declares that he had done his utmost to escape a burden which his state of health evidently showed he was unable to support, but that it had been forced upon him at very short notice, and he had so little expected it that he hardly knew what his duties as Prolocutor were, or what was expected of him.

A fortnight later he received his last piece of preferment. This was the Vicarage of St. Dunstan's in the West, which had been promised him some years before by Richard Sackville, Earl of Dorset, one of the most munificent patrons of poets and men of letters in that munificent age.

.   .   .   .   .   .

St. Dunstan's had been held for fifty years by Dr. Thomas White, who had come up to London shortly after taking his degree at Oxford, and been presented to St. Dunstan's in 1575, *i.e.* two years after Donne was born. Here he attracted the notice of Bishop Aylmer by his eloquence as a preacher, and in the year of the Armada he became Prebend of Mora in St. Paul's Cathedral. During the next five years he was promoted in rapid succession to the Chancellorship of Salisbury, to a Canonry at Christ Church, Oxford, and to another in the Chapel Royal at Windsor. All these preferments he held till his death, on the 1st of March 1624, and it must be admitted that he made a good use of the wealth he acquired. Besides building and endowing almshouses at Bristol, where he was born, he founded Sion College in his lifetime, and the Professorship of Moral Philosophy at Oxford, which still bears his name, and he provided for the endowment of a Lectureship at St. Dunstan's, the lecturer being required to preach every Sunday and Thursday afternoon.

From its proximity to the Temple and the lawyers' quarter, and within a short walk of most of the great houses of the nobility, St. Dunstan's could not fail to be a very important cure for any man of earnestness and more than ordinary gifts as a preacher; it had been for long what is now called a *fashionable* church, and Donne felt the responsibility which was laid upon him. The income was not large, but it was not so inconsiderable as might be inferred from a passage in one of his letters, where he says, " I make not a shilling profit of St. Dunstan's as a churchman," meaning that, after payment of all outgoings and the stipend of his curate, there was nothing left out of the *vicarial* tithes. As to the *rectorial* tithes, of these he held a lease from the Earl of Dorset at a rent which apparently was higher than it should have been. It is abundantly clear that Donne accepted the living of St. Dunstan's from no mercenary motive. He seems to have had a desire to bring himself into closer personal relations with his congregation than was possible at St. Paul's. There he had nothing that could be strictly called a cure of souls. The "statutable sermons" preached in the Cathedral brought him no nearer to the people who came to listen; there was a gulf between him and them—he was not their pastor, and they were not his flock. At St. Dunstan's all this was changed. Though continuing, of course, to reside at the deanery, he appears to have given up the vicarage-house to his *lecturer* as curate; this was Matthew Griffith, a young

man who had but recently taken his M.A. degree at
Oxford, and for whom he is said to have entertained
a warm regard.   Mr. Griffith suffered for his loyalty
during the Commonwealth days ; he became eventually
Preacher at the Temple, and held one of the City livings
in the gift of the Dean and Chapter, from which he
was ejected as a Royalist in 1642.   At the Restoration he recovered his benefice, and died there in 1665.

Donne preached his first sermon at St. Dunstan's on
the 11th April, and chose as his text Deut. xxv. 5 :
" *If brethren dwell together, and one of them die, and
leave no child, the wife of the dead shall not marry
without unto a stranger : her husband's brother shall go
in unto her, and take her to him to wife, and perform the
duty of the husband's brother to her.*"

The sermon is a kind of manifesto setting forth the
preacher's view of the reciprocal duties of the pastor
and his flock.   It was evidently composed with great
care, and is expressed in language almost homely in
its simplicity, very unlike the ordinary style of
Donne's most studied sermons delivered on important
occasions.   " From these words," he says, "we shall
make our approaches and application to the present
occasion. . . . First, there is a marriage in the case—
the taking and leaving the Church is not an indifferent,
an arbitrary thing; it is a marriage, and marriage
implies honour ; it is an honourable estate, and that
implies charge ; it is a burdensome state—there is
honour and labour in marriage.   *You* must be content
to afford the honour, *we* must be content to endure
the labour. . . . It is a marriage after the death of
another. . . . It must be a brother, a spiritual brother
—a professor of the same faith—that succeeds in this

marriage, in this possession, and this government of
that widow Church. . . . And then, being thus
married to this widow—taking the charge of this
Church—he must 'perform the duty of a husband's
brother.' *He* must—it is a personal service, not to be
done always by proxy and delegates ; he *must*, and he
must *perform*—not begin well and not persist, com-
mence and not consummate ; but perform the work—as
it is a duty. . . . It is a duty in us to do that we
are sent for, by His word and His sacraments to
establish you in His holy obedience and His rich and
honourable service, . . . and that the true right of
people and pastor and patron be preserved, to the
preservation of love and peace and good opinion of one
another."

In the course of the sermon all these points are
dwelt on, and he ends by emphasising and recapitu-
lating what he had said. "If the pastor love, there
will be a double labour ; if the people love, there will
be double respect. For where the congregation loves
the pastor, he will forbear bitter reproofs and wounding
increpations, and where the pastor loves his congregation, his rebukes, because they proceed out of love, will
be acceptable and well interpreted by them, . . . that
love being the root of all, the fruit of all may be peace ;
love being the soul of all, the body of all may be
unity, which the Lord of unity and concord grant to
us all for His Son Jesus Christ's sake."

Such was Donne's manifesto when he preached for
the first time in St. Dunstan's pulpit ; it was a noble
setting forth of a high ideal, which for the remaining
seven years of his life he strove with all his heart to
carry out, and in doing so he found his reward.

The fact that no more than five or six sermons preached at St. Dunstan's are to be found among Donne's printed works [1] goes far to prove that his usual practice in that church was to trust to such notes as he had prepared beforehand. In preaching at court, or on the important occasions when he was called upon to speak with authority, and when every word had to be weighed lest any word should be misunderstood or misinterpreted, he doubtless committed the sermon to memory, according to the almost universal custom of the time; and of such sermons we may assume that we have the *ipsissima verba* of the preacher, who was liable to be called to account for them, and sometimes to produce the manuscript, which might be used against him; indeed this happened once to Donne himself, as we shall see a little later on.

Not many months before Donne's becoming Vicar of St. Dunstan's, Izaak Walton had married his first wife, and settled as a tradesman in the parish. He was then in his thirty-first year, and he occupied a house on the north side of Fleet Street, two doors to the west of Chancery Lane. [2]

A close intimacy sprang up between the gentle angler and Donne. On the one side there was an almost idolatrous reverence and admiration; on the other a generous esteem and affection. From this time Walton's life of his friend and pastor is much more to be trusted than the earlier portion, where many

[1] In the first folio there are eighty sermons; in the second, fifty; in the third, twenty-five; to these must be added five others (including that at the funeral of Lady Danvers), published during Donne's lifetime, four of which have never been reprinted.

[2] There is an engraving of Nash's drawing of Walton's house in Zouch's *Life of Walton*, p. 4, 12mo, 1823.

errors of detail are to be found which modern
research has corrected; and Walton's account of
Donne's habits and of his inner life and character
(which became increasingly softened and sanctified
during his declining years) gives us a picture such as
no other writer in the English language has put into
words. Walton's life of Donne is the masterpiece of
biographical literature. It is curious to note how, in
the latter portion of this inimitable sketch of his great
friend, Walton seems to think of him much less as
Dean of St. Paul's than as the honoured Vicar of St.
Dunstan's, and how he represents him from the day
when he entered upon his new vocation of parish
priest as becoming more and more absorbed in that,
as though the claims which St. Paul's had upon him
were regarded as official duties indeed, but such as
were of secondary importance as compared with those
more personal calls upon him which his parish and his
parishioners claimed at his hands. Indeed, from this
time Donne retired more and more from the old
world in which for the last twenty years he had been
such a conspicuous figure, and he rarely attended the
court except on those occasions when he was summoned
to preach in his turn as one of the king's chaplains;
and though the long and close friendships which he had
formed with many of the nobility still brought him
necessarily into frequent intercourse with some of the
greatest people in the land,—by whom, as by the
members of their families, he was regarded as one
worthy of special confidence and true regard,—yet the
tone of his letters is different from that of his earlier
correspondence; there is little of mere court gossip
and laboured compliments, the old frivolity has died

out, and the old anxiety about the future. The world had not treated him badly. God had been very gracious to him. The work that he had to do he loved to perform. Riches, he knew—and had again and again proclaimed it—were as often as not a snare. He aimed at nothing higher than he had attained to ; he asked for no more than had been bestowed.

"The latter part of his life," says Walton, "may be said to be a continual study ; for as he usually preached once a week, if not oftener, so after his sermon he never gave his eyes rest till he had chosen out a new text, and that night cast his sermon into a form, and his text into divisions ; and the next day betook himself to consult the fathers and so commit his meditations to his memory, which was excellent. But upon Saturday he usually gave himself and his mind a rest from the weary burden of his week's meditations, and usually spent that day in visitation of friends, or some other diversions of his thoughts, and would say that he gave both his body and mind that refreshment that he might be enabled to do the work of the day following, not faintly, but with courage and cheerfulness."

.   .   .   .   .   .

When Donne entered upon his ministry at St. Dunstan's the reign of James I. was drawing to a close, and Prince Charles had returned to England. When Lord Bristol took his leave of Philip IV. on 28th January 1624, the long-protracted negotiations concerned with the Spanish marriage practically came to an end. James was compelled to assemble Parliament once more ; and on the 23rd of March, in deference to the strong feeling expressed in the House of Commons, the king declared the treaties dissolved. Meanwhile, the feeling in the country at large against the popish recusants and the Roman propagandists was waxing stronger and stronger. To tolerate them or their tenets was denounced as abominable. Yet the Prince of Wales was still unmarried, and it was obviously desirable that a consort for him should be provided without delay. On the 17th May, Hay, Earl of Carlisle, was sent to France to negotiate a treaty of marriage with Henrietta Maria; and, as before, the great difficulty that presented itself was the question of how the English Catholics were to be treated in the future. Certain concessions were made which were very distasteful to the people, and especially to the Puritans, and it is possible that, among other sufficient reasons, the desire to avoid the discussion of the subject in the House of Commons may have suggested successive prorogations of Parliament from the 29th May till its final reassembling on the 19th February 1625. The treaty for the marriage of Prince Charles to Henrietta Maria had been previously ratified by James I. on the 12th December 1624, though nearly five months passed before it was actually carried into effect.

That spring was a very sickly season, and among others of the nobility who succumbed was the Marquis of Hamilton, who on the 2nd March died at Whitehall of what is called "a malignant fever," and which was probably either typhus, or perhaps the dreaded plague, which a month later began its frightful ravages in London. Chamberlain speaks of Hamilton as "the flower of that nation" (Scotland), and "the gallantest gentleman of both nations." He was little more than thirty-five years of age, and a man of great ability and promise. His death was a painful shock to the king, and some days after it occurred Sir Robert Carr wrote to Donne asking him to write a poem upon the occasion. He could hardly refuse, and he sent the following letter in reply:—

"SIR,—I presume you rather try what you can do in me, than what I can do in verse: you know my uttermost when it was best, and even then I did best when I had least truth for my subjects. In this present case there is so much truth as it defeats all poetry. Call, therefore, this paper by what name you will, and if it be not worthy of him, nor of you, nor of me, smother it, and be that the sacrifice. If you had commanded me to have waited on his body in Scotland and preached there, I would have embraced the obligation with more alacrity. But I thank you, that you would command to do that which I was loth to do, for even that hath given a tincture of merit to the obedience of
"Your poor friend and servant in Christ Jesus,
"J. DONNE."

Donne put his thoughts into the form of what he calls "A Hymn to the Saints and to Marquis Hamilton." It was at once circulated in manuscript, but so strong was the prejudice at this time against a divine stooping so low as to write poetry, that Chamberlain, when forwarding a copy of "certain verses of our Dean of Paul's upon the death of the Marquis of Hamilton," adds, that "though they be reasonable, witty, and well done, yet I could wish

a man of his years and place to give over versifying."
One would have thought that the beautiful conclusion
of the poem might have protected the writer from
any word of disparagement—

> "And if, fair soul, not with first *Innocents*
> Thy station be, but with the *Penitents*,
>
> . . . .
>
> When thou rememb'rest what sins thou didst find
> Amongst those many friends now left behind,
> And seest such sinners as they are, with thee
> Got thither by repentance, let it be
> Thy wish to wish all there, to wish them clean ;
> Wish him a David, her a Magdalen."

A few days after Lord Hamilton's death the king
became alarmingly ill at Theobalds. The physicians
soon pronounced the symptoms very grave, and on
Sunday the 27th of the month he breathed his last ;
Prince Charles, his successor, being at his side. The
new king was proclaimed the same day at Whitehall,
and immediately started for London, where he took up
his residence at St. James's Palace. Donne received
a command to preach in the chapel there next
Sunday, and the king attended, "his majesty looking
very pale, his visage being the true glass of his inward,
as well as his accoutrements of external mourning."

Donne chose his text from the 11th Psalm, ver. 3 :
"*If the foundations be destroyed, what can the righteous
do ?*" It was a noble, outspoken, and pathetic
sermon. It was not published till some months after
its delivery, and has never been reprinted, though it
deserves to be reckoned among the preacher's most
ingenious and splendid efforts. The body of James I.
was removed to Denmark House on the 4th April.

While it lay there in state Donne was again called upon to preach in the chapel on the 27th April " to the nobility," who composed the congregation.

A greater contrast than this beautiful sermon offers to the fulsome and almost profane oration which the Bishop of Lincoln (Williams) delivered at Westminster Abbey, can hardly be imagined.

While the late king's body was lying unburied at Denmark House, the plague " had once more settled down upon the capital." Isolated cases had been reported on the bills of mortality as early as February, but from the third week in March they went on slowly increasing in numbers week by week. Parliament assembled on the 18th June, and continued sitting till the 11th July. That week more than a thousand deaths in eighty-two infected parishes of London were attributed to the plague alone, and, the outlook being serious, the House of Commons was adjourned till the 1st of August, when it was summoned to meet at Oxford. But in London the pestilence increased its area and its ravages. In the months of August and September upwards of 26,000 poor wretches were carried out to their horrible burial-places, and it is stated that in the 119 parishes within and without the walls and liberties of the city, during the year, at least 41,313 fell victims to the awful visitation. In the parish of Stepney alone there were nearly 500 plague deaths in a single week. The parish of St. Dunstan's, though one of the smallest in the city, suffered frightfully, and no less than 642 deaths are recorded as having been caused by the plague during this year in that little area, where in our own times it is thought that a population of 1860 souls is quite overcrowded. The adjournment of the House of Commons was the signal for a general exodus from London. By the middle of August the nobility, the magistrates, and all who were rich enough to go away, had left the city to take care of itself. "The magistrates in desperation," writes one, "have abandoned every care: everyone does what he pleases, and the houses of merchants who have left London are broken into and robbed."

Dr. Meadows, Rector of St. Gabriel, Fenchurch Street, who nobly stuck to his post, though a man no longer young, writing on the 1st September, says: "The want and misery is the greatest here that ever any man living knew: no trading at all; the rich all gone; housekeepers and apprentices of manual trades begging in the streets, and that in such a lamentable manner as will make the hearts of the strongest to yearn." In one of Mead's news-letters, he tells how "A gentleman who on Thursday was sennight came through the city at one o'clock in the afternoon, resembled the face thereof, at that time, to the appearance it useth to have at three o'clock in the morning in the month of June: no more people stirring, no more shops open. The citizens fled away as out of a house on fire, and stuffed their pockets with their best wares, and threw themselves into the highways, and were not received so much as into barns, and perished so; some of them with more money about them than would have bought the village where they died. A justice of the peace told me of one that had died so with £1400 about him."

It is not to be wondered at if during that dreadful autumn the churches were closed for lack of congrega-

tions; and Donne appears to have remained in London
till the end of November, about which time the
pestilence was almost at its worse, and it is probable
that the report of his death which was circulated
about this time originated in his having kept to his
post through the worst days of the contagion, and the
fact that he had not been seen for many weeks in the
great houses of his noble friends gave credibility to
the rumour.   In a letter of the 21st December
he gives the following account of himself and his
movements :—

"SIR,—Our blessed Saviour, who abounds in power
and goodness towards us all, bless you, and your
family, with blessings proportioned to His ends in you
all, and bless you with the testimony of a rectified
conscience, of having discharged all the offices of a
father, towards your discreet and worthy daughters,
and bless them with a satisfaction, and quiescence, and
more, with a complacency and a joy, in good ends, and
ways towards them, Amen.

"Your man brought me your letter of the 8th of
December this 21st of the same, to Chelsea, and gives
me the largeness, till Friday to send a letter to Paul's-
house.   There can scarce be any piece of that, or
of those things whereof you require light from me,
that is not come to your knowledge, by some clearer
way, between the time of your letter and this.   Besides, the report of my death hath thus much of truth
in it, that though I be not dead, yet I am buried.
Within a few weeks after I immured myself in this
house, the infection struck into the town, into so many
houses as that it became ill-manners to make any

visits. Therefore, I never went to Knoll,[1] nor Hanworth,[2] nor Keyston, nor to the court, since the court came into these quarters, nor am yet come to London : therefore I am little able to give you account of high stages. . . .

"Mr. George Herbert is here at the receipt of your letter, and with his service to you, tells you that all of Uvedall-house are well. I reserve not the mention of my Lady Huntingdon to the end of my letter, as grains to make the gold weight, but as tincture to make the better gold, when you find room to intrude so poor and impertinent a name, as mine is, in her presence. I beseech you let her ladyship know that she hath sowed her favour towards me, in such a ground, that if I be grown better (as I hope I am) her favours are grown with me, and though they were great when she conferred them, yet (if I mend every day) they increase in me every day, and therefore every day multiply my thankfulness towards her ladyship : say what you will (if you like not this expression) that may make her ladyship know that I shall never let fall the memory, nor the just valuation of her noble favours to me, nor leave them unrequited in my exchequer, which is the blessings of God upon my prayers. If I should write another sheet, I should be able to serve your curiosity no more of dukes nor lords nor courts, and this half line serves to tell you that I am truly

"Your poor friend and humble servant in Christ Jesus,   J. DONNE."

This letter was written from Lady Danvers' house,

[1] Knole Park, Lord Dorset's house.   [2] Hanworth, Lord Carlisle's.

where he was evidently staying; and another letter
from the same place, written somewhat earlier, gives
us some dreadful particulars of terror and demoralisa-
tion which the plague had caused among the Londoners.
So it was at St. Dunstan's, where the mortality
continued its ravages even after it had begun to abate
in larger parishes. As the winter drew on the plague
abated, and on the 15th January 1626 Donne
preached at St. Dunstan's on Ex. xii. 30 : " *For there
was not a house where there was not one dead.*" He
calls it " The first sermon after our dispersion by the
sickness." It was a pathetic and impressive sermon,
elaborate as usual, but admirably suited to the
occasion. It is one of the few sermons preached at
St. Dunstan's that Donne thought it advisable to
write out fully before delivering. He knew that on
such an occasion much would be expected from him,
and a sense of responsibility doubtless led him to
bestow upon it more than usual pains and careful
preparation. Twelve times at least, during 1626,
Donne was called upon to preach what he calls
" solemn sermons to great auditories at Paul's and at
court." All save one are to be found in the folios or
the collected edition of his works.

One has somehow escaped notice. It was
preached before Charles I. at Whitehall, and was
immediately published by command of the king. The
text[1] (Isa. l. 1) was a strange one, and gave very
little promise of what was coming : the sermon was a

---

[1] " *Thus saith the Lord, Where is the bill of your mother's divorcement, whom I have put away? Or which of my creditors is it to whom
I have sold you? Behold, for your iniquities have ye sold yourselves,
and for your transgressions is your mother put away.*"

vehement denunciation of the hateful doctrine of *Reprobation*, which some of the extreme Calvinists were talking much about at this time, and which Donne abhorred and frequently lifted up his voice against. As the sermon is a very characteristic one and is very little known, I venture to dwell upon it here at some length. " In this text," he says, " there are two parts : God's discharge from all imputation of tyranny, and man's discharge from all necessity of perishing." The mother is the Church, and God's putting away of this mother is the leaving her to herself. " That Church which now enjoys so abundantly Truth and Unity may be perished with heresy and wounded with schism, and yet God be free from all imputation of tyranny. . . . 'Tis true there may be a selling, there may be a putting away, but hath not God reserved to Himself a power of revocation in both —in all cases ?

" Where is the bill of thy mother's divorcement— *Ubi libellus ?* Where is this bill ? Upon what do ye ground this jealousy and suspicion in God that He should divorce you ? It must be God's whole book, and not a few misunderstood sentences out of that book, that must try thee. . . . Those bills of divorcement were to be authentically sealed—*Ubi iste libellus ?* Hath thy imaginary bill of divorce and everlasting separation from God any seal from Him ? God hath given thee seals of His mercy in both His sacraments, but seals of reprobation at first, or of irrevocable separation now, there are none from God. . . . No calamity—not temporal ; no ! not spiritual. No darkness in the understanding, no scruple in the conscience, no perplexity in the resolution. Not a sudden death,

12

not a shameful death, not a stupid, not a raging death,
must be to thyself by the way, or may be to us,
who may see thine end, an evidence, a seal of eternal
reprobation or of final separation. . . . If the bill
were interlined or blotted or dropt, the bill was
void—*Ubi libellus?* What place of Scripture soever
thou pretend, that place is interlined—interlined by
the Spirit of God Himself with conditions and limitations and provisions,—'If thou return,' 'if thou
repent,'—and that interlining destroys the bill. And
canst thou think that that God who married thee in
the *house of dust,* and married thee in the house of
infirmity, and divorced thee not then (He made thee
not no creature, nor He made thee not no man),
having now married thee in the house of power, and
of peace, in the body of His Son, the Church, will now
divorce thee ? Lastly, to end this consideration of
divorces, if the bill were interlined or blotted or
dropt, the bill was void—*Ubi libellus?* What
place of Scripture soever thou pretend, that place
is interlined—interlined by the Spirit of God Himself
with conditions and limitations and provisions,—'If
thou repent, if thou return,'—and that interlining
destroys the bill.

"Look also if this bill be not dropt upon and
blotted; the venom of the serpent is dropt upon
it, the wormwood of thy desperation is dropt upon
it, the gall of thy melancholy is dropt upon it; and
that voids the bill. If thou canst not discern these
drops before, drop upon it now ; drop the tears of true
compunction, drop the blood of thy Saviour; and that
voids the bill; and through that spectacle, the blood
of thy Saviour, look upon that bill, and thou shalt

see that that bill was nailed to the cross when He was nailed, and torn when His body was torn ; and that hath cancelled the bill."

Another sermon of Donne's during this year was that which he preached at the funeral of Sir William Cokayne, who was buried in St. Paul's on the 12th of December. Sir William was a London merchant who had accumulated an enormous fortune, and was one of the richest men in England. His lady was Mary, daughter of Richard Morris, who had been Master of the Ironmongers' Company in 1588, *i.e.* fourteen years before Donne's father had served the same honourable office. Her ladyship and Donne were born in the same year. In childhood they must have been playmates, for their respective homes were hardly more than a bow-shot apart ; but whether anything in their later lives had brought them together again we are not told. What we do know is that during Donne's last years, and when the hand of death was upon him, he was corresponding on very close and affectionate terms with the forsaken wife of the eccentric Thomas Cokayne and mother of Sir Aston Cokayne, the poet ; but there is nothing to show that there were any very cordial relations between these Cokaynes and the far more prosperous branch of the same family. In preaching Sir William Cokayne's funeral sermon Donne speaks of him as a personal friend. He chose for his text John xi. 21 : " *Lord, if Thou hadst been here, my brother had not died.*" The sermon is a very interesting one for the little incidents which it gives us in the life of the dead man which are illustrative of the manners of the time ; and one passage indicates that the choir of St. Paul's had continued to be reserved for the prebendaries and clergy exclusively, long after the changes brought about by Henry VIII. Speaking of the dignified and devout bearing of the City magnates during their attendance at the cathedral, Donne says: " And truly . . . that reverence that they use in this place, when they come hither, is that that makes us who have now the administration of this choir, glad *that our predecessors, but a very few years before our time (and not before all our times), admitted these honourable and worshipful persons of this city to sit in this choir, so as they do upon Sundays*; the Church receives an honour in it ; but the honour is more in their reverence than in their presence."

The two points upon which Donne dwells very eloquently in this sermon are—" First, that there is nothing in this world perfect, and then that, such as it is, there is nothing constant, nothing permanent. . . . What one thing do we *know* perfectly ?   Almost all knowledge is rather like a child that is embalmed to make a mummy, than that that is nursed to make a man ; rather conserved in the stature of the first age, than grown to be greater ; and if there be any addition to knowledge, it is rather a new knowledge than a greater knowledge ; rather a singularity in a desire of proposing something that was not known at all before, than an improving, an advancing, a multiplying of former inceptions ; and by that means no knowledge comes to be perfect. . . .

" But when we consider with a religious seriousness the manifold weaknesses of the strongest devotions in time of prayer, it is a sad consideration.   I throw myself down in my chamber, and I call in and invite God and His angels thither ; and when they are there,

I neglect God and His angels for the noise of a fly, for the rattling of a coach, for the whining of a door; I talk on, in the same posture of prayer; eyes lifted up, knees bowed down, as though I prayed to God; and if God should ask me when I thought last of God in that prayer I cannot tell: sometimes I find that I forgot what I was about, but when I began to forget it, I cannot tell. A memory of yesterday's pleasures, a fear of to-morrow's dangers, a straw under my knee, a noise in mine ear, a chimera in my brain, troubles me in my prayer. So certainly is there nothing, nothing in spiritual things, perfect in this world. . . . Weaknesses there were in those holy and devout sisters of Lazarus. . . . Our devotions do not the less bear us upright in the sight of God, because they have some declinations towards natural affections. God doth easilier pardon some neglecting of His grace when it proceeds out of a tenderness, or may be excused out of good nature, than any presuming upon His grace.

.   .   .   .

"And since we are in an action of preparing this dead brother of ours to that state . . . so shall we dismiss you with an occasional inverting the text from passion in Martha's mouth to joy in ours—' *Lord, because Thou wast here, our brother is not dead.*'

.   .   .   .   .   .

"In the presence of God we lay him down. In the power of God he shall rise. In the person of Christ he is risen already. And so into the same hands that have received his soul, we commend his body; beseeching His blessed Spirit that . . . for all our sakes, but especially for His own glory, He will be pleased to hasten the consummation of all, in that kingdom which that Son of God hath purchased for us, with the inestimable price of His incorruptible blood."

Donne closed the year 1626 by preaching his usual Christmas Day sermon at St. Paul's, and he began the next year by preaching there one of his prebend sermons in January.

CHAPTER VIII

A YEAR OF GLOOM

WHEN the year 1627 opened there was only one prominent divine in England who can in any sense be called a great preacher; and that one was the Dean of St. Paul's. Bishop Andrewes died in September 1626. Among the bishops that survived there was not a man who had any popular gifts or who attracted any large following. Abbot was always solemn and dull. Laud was always hard and dry. Montagu, not yet a bishop, was a controversialist pure and simple. Williams was impossible. Ussher only appeared in England at wide intervals; his immense reputation had not yet travelled far from Ireland, though scholars could not speak of him too highly. Sanderson had not yet attracted the notice of Laud, and, sound and solid as his sermons were, he was the first of our eminent theologians who never trusted himself in the pulpit without his manuscript. Such a mere *reader* was not likely to be run after by the multitude. As for Joseph Hall, who was consecrated Bishop of Exeter this year, he was everything except great: pre-eminently clever, ingenious to a fault, a born *journalist* with a graceful pen and a fluent tongue, he was never at a loss for a retort or an epigram; but whereas Andrewes declared of himself that "whenever he preached twice in a day he *prated* once," Hall boasts that his regular practice at Waltham was to preach three sermons every week—and we may be sure it was always very pleasant prattle. At Cambridge there was one young man of whom the world would hear something by and by, but Jeremy Taylor was now only in his teens.

Donne as a preacher stood alone. It was said of him that he was always growing more impressive and more eloquent as he grew older—the truth being that he became ever more and more absorbed in the duties of his sacred office, throwing his whole heart into it, rising to every occasion on which demands were made upon him, always doing his best as an enthusiast with a mission, who felt that he would have to give account for the talent that was committed to him.

We moderns have lost touch with the pulpit oratory of the seventeenth century, and it is difficult for those who have never acquired any familiarity with the sermons of the Jacobean era to understand the effect they produced upon mixed congregations. In the way Holy Scripture was dealt with by the preachers of that day, there was, to our taste, a quite fantastic ingenuity that we are apt to think meretricious.

These men handled Holy Scripture in their sermons after a method which had the sanction of ages of traditionary interpretation. Whatever could be read into a text, or whatever could be drawn out of it, was regarded as perfectly legitimate. It was done with such consummate rhetorical art that congregations were dazzled and bewildered: they took it all very seriously; we are inclined to regard it as mere trickery, and often find it hard to believe that there was not a sophistical unreality about it all. Never-theless, history shows that in every age the orators have reached the hearts and consciences of the thousands, where the logicians have hardly convinced the tens. The cold light of dialectics leaves men where it found them,—" Ice makes no conflagration ! " When argument has done its utmost, then comes the fervid enthusiast with his flaming sword that turns every way, and at its touch the unreasoning emotions are fanned into a glowing heat. The startled multitude never doubts that the fire has been kindled by a spark from the altar of God. It takes the prophet at his own estimation, and accepts his premises without demur, and in those premises astounding conclusions are involved. Granted that every syllable and every letter in the printed pages of the Old Testament and of the New found its place there by divine inspiration and carries with it a divine authority, and what a tremendous power the preacher had at his disposal! Fortified with that, he became at once a prophet armed with a message from the Most High; the torrent of denunciation, ex-postulation, warning, pleading, menace, or assurance and encouragement poured forth resistless from lips that spake the very truth; the sinner might be scared, the saint be lifted up to the seventh heaven,—neither presumed to criticise. ." Yea ! hath not God said ? "

What gave a double-force to Donne's preaching was, that everyone knew he had no ambition for any higher preferment—that he was giving his best to the ministry of the Word—that he was labouring very much more than he was required to do. The

noble earnestness of his manner, the wide sympathy and enormous learning, the sound judgment
and large-hearted tolerance, won men's confidence;
and the bursts of eloquence that startled his
hearers so often when they came quite unexpectedly
upon them, attracted crowds to listen whenever it
was announced that he was going to appear in the
pulpit. But no man in so prominent a position as he,
could hope to find all his audience friendly. There
were gainsayers and critics who were on the watch
for him; and never, whether in politics or religion,
were the factions more embittered against one another,
nor was it ever more difficult to avoid giving offence
when a man believed with all his heart, and felt that he
had a message to deliver which he could not keep back.

It was in this year, 1627, that that incident
occurred which Izaak Walton has strangely antedated by some four or five years, and when he tells
us that his friend "was once, and but once, clouded
with the king's displeasure." The circumstances
were these :—

Dr. Richard Montagu, a Cambridge man, and one of
the most acute and learned scholars of his day, had
during the last few years of King James's reign made
himself famous by advocating in a very caustic and
trenchant style a somewhat novel view of the position
which he claimed for the Church of England as a
true branch of the Catholic Church, whose doctrines
were opposed to the teaching of the Church of Rome
on the one hand, and equally opposed to those of
Geneva on the other. He found himself, as a matter
of course, the object of rancorous denunciations on
the part of the Calvinist sectaries and the Puritan

clergy; while their allies among the laity were scarcely less bitterly opposed to him for his vigorous support of extreme views of the royal prerogative. On the 11th February 1626 a conference was arranged at Buckingham House for the discussion of the questions at issue between Montagu and his opponents. Dr. White, Dean of Carlisle, undertook to defend what may be called the High Church views. Morton, Donne's old and dear friend, now Bishop of Lichfield, and Dr. Preston, who had succeeded Donne as Preacher at Lincoln's Inn, were chosen to assail those views from the Low Church side. The conference, as usual, came to an abortive termination; and Charles I., tired of the business, issued a proclamation forbidding any further disputation on the abstruse questions under discussion. A year before this, Montagu had written his famous *Appello Cæsarem*; and when Archbishop Abbot, after reading the work, had stoutly refused to license it, it was printed in spite of him, under the imprimatur of Dr. White, the aforesaid Dean of Carlisle.

In April 1627 Donne was appointed to preach at Whitehall before the king. Laud, then Bishop of Bath and Wells, was in attendance. He was, as might have been expected, the strongest of all Montagu's supporters, and he was daily gaining more and more influence over Charles. He could hardly have helped feeling some suspicion of Donne, who was on intimate terms with Abbot, and was the much-loved friend of Morton, with whom he had been a fellow-labourer in his theological studies for well-nigh thirty years. What line would the author of the *Pseudo Martyr* take—the divine who had been honoured with a medal by the Synod of Dort eight years before?

Donne chose as his text Mark iv. 24: " *Take heed what ye hear.*" It is difficult to conceive how any unprejudiced hearer could have been able to discover ground for offence in the beautiful and wise sermon which he preached; but where men come to find fault, they will not fail to discover it. It is more charitable, perhaps, to suppose that some of those present may have honestly misunderstood the preacher, but, after carefully reading the sermon several times, I can find only one passage that may have hurt the prejudices or irritated the susceptibilities of some of the audience as possibly reflecting upon themselves:—

"When the apostles came in their peregrinations to a new state, to a new court, to Rome itself, they did not inquire, 'How stands the Emperor affected to Christ and to the preaching of the gospel? Is there not a sister or a wife that might be wrought upon to further the preaching of Christ? Are there not some persons great in power and place that might be content to hold a party together by admitting the preaching of Christ?' This was not their way. All divinity that is bespoken, and not ready made, fitted to certain turns and not to general ends, and all divines that have their souls and consciences so disposed as their libraries may be,—at *that* end stand Papists, and at that end Protestants, and *he* in the middle, as near one as the other,—all these have a brackish taste as a river hath that comes near the sea; so have they in coming near the sea of Rome."

Whether this passage were the one that was found fault with or not, Donne had scarcely got home to the deanery before he was startled by learning that he had grievously displeased the king. The intelligence came to him in a letter from Sir Robert Carr. In acknowledging this, Donne writes as follows:—

"A few hours after I had the honour of your letter, I had another from my Lord of Bath and Wells, commanding from the king a copy of my sermon. I am in preparations of that, with diligence, yet this morning I waited upon his lordship, and laid up in him this truth, that of the Bishop of Canterbury's sermon, to this hour, I never heard syllable, nor what way, nor upon what points he went: and for mine, it was put into that very order, in which I delivered it, more than two months since. Freely to you I say, I would I were a little more guilty: only mine innocency makes me afraid. I hoped for the king's approbation heretofore in many of my sermons, and I have had it; but yesterday I came very near looking for thanks, for in my life I was never in any one piece so studious of his service; therefore, exceptions being taken, and displeasure kindled at this, I am afraid it was rather brought thither, than met there. If you know any more, fit for me (because I hold that unfit for me, to appear in my master's sight as long as this cloud hangs, and therefore this day forbear my ordinary waitings), I beseech you to intimate it to

"Your very humble and very thankful servant,

"J. DONNE."

The next letter enters into further particulars:—

To the Right Honourable SIR ROBERT CARR, *at Court.*[1]

"SIR,—I was this morning at your door, somewhat early; and I am put into such a distaste of my last sermon, as that I dare not practise any part of it, and therefore though I said then, that we are bound to speak aloud, though we awaken men, and make them froward, yet after two or three modest knocks at the door, I went away. Yet I understood after, the king was gone abroad, and thought you might be gone with him. I came to give you an account of that, which this does as well. I have now put into my Lord of Bath and Wells' hands the sermon faithfully exscribed. I beseech you be pleased to hearken farther after it; I am still upon my jealousy, that the king brought thither some disaffection towards me, grounded upon some other demerit of mine, and took it not from the sermon. For, as Cardinal Cusanus writ a book *Cribratio Alcorani,* I have cribrated, and re-cribrated, and post-cribrated the sermon, and must necessarily say, the king who hath let fall his eye upon some of my poems, never saw, of mine, a hand, or an eye, or an affection, set down with so much study, and diligence, and labour of syllables, as in this sermon I expressed those two points, which I take so much to conduce to his service, the imprinting of persuasibility and obedience in the subject, and the breaking of the bed of whisperers, by casting in a bone, of making them suspect and distrust one another. I remember I heard the old king say of a good sermon, that he thought the preacher never had thought of his sermon, till he spoke it; it seemed to

[1] About 1624.—ED.

him negligently and extemporally spoken. And I knew that he had weighed every syllable, for half a year before, which made me conclude, that the king had before some prejudice upon him. So, the best of my hope is, that some over bold allusions, or expressions in the way, might divert his majesty, from vouchsafing to observe the frame and purpose of the sermon. When he sees the general scope, I hope his goodness will pardon collateral escapes. I entreated the bishop to ask his majesty, whether his displeasure extended so far, as that I should forbear waiting, and appearing in his presence; and I had a return, that I might come. Till I had that, I would not offer to put myself under your roof. To-day I come for that purpose, to say prayers. And if, in any degree, my health suffer it, I shall do so, to-morrow. If anything fall into your observation before that (because the bishop is likely to speak to the king of it, perchance, this night), if it amount to such an increase of displeasure, as that it might be unfit for me to appear, I beseech you afford me the knowledge. Otherwise, I am likely to inquire of you personally, to-morrow before nine in the morning, and to put into your presence then,

"Your very humble, and very true, and very honest servant to God and the king and you,

"J. DONNE.

"I writ yesterday to my Lord Duke, by my Lord Carlisle, who assured me of a gracious acceptation of my putting myself in his protection."

The king had no sooner read the sermon and listened to the explanation offered than Donne was at once restored to favour, and for the remainder of his

life continued to receive assurances of the confidence
and esteem which Charles felt for his favourite chaplain.   Donne's last sermon was preached before the
king at Whitehall, a few weeks before his death, as
· we shall see in the sequel.

In June of this year he lost one of his oldest and
most faithful friends, Lady Danvers, better known by
the name of Magdalen Herbert.   Her first husband,
Richard Herbert of Montgomery Castle, died in 1596,
leaving her a widow with ten children, of whom
Edward, Lord Herbert of Cherbury, was the eldest,
and the saintly George Herbert, the fifth son.   She
remained a widow for twelve years, and then married,
in 1608, Sir John Danvers, who was little more than
twenty years old.   He was a young inan of great
wealth, and kept up a style of living at Danvers
House, Chelsea, which even in that age was looked
upon as extraordinarily sumptuous.   Here Donne was
a frequent visitor, and always welcome.   Lady Danvers was noted for her exemplary life and bountiful
charities.   She had been in failing health for some
time, and in May 1627 her son George Herbert was
summoned to her side.   She lingered on till the first
week in June, when she died, and was buried in
Chelsea Church on the 8th of that month, without
the usual sermon.   Donne had been asked to perform
this duty, but, being "bound by pre-obligations and
pre-contracts to his own profession," it had to be post-
poned till the 1st July, when an immense congregation
assembled to hear the great preacher.

Before giving out his text [2 Peter iii. 13] he
offered up one of those glorious acts of prayer and
adoration with which on several occasions he prefaced

his most notable sermons. The opening words must have come upon those that heard them with a surprise that could never be forgotten :—

"O eternal and most glorious God! enable us in life and death seriously to consider the price of a soul. . . . Suffer us not, therefore, O Lord, so to undervalue ourselves, nay, so to impoverish Thee, as to give away those souls, Thy souls, Thy dear and precious souls, for nothing!"

But no words can adequately express the sublime elevation of tone in this wonderful prayer—the majestic sweep and rhythm of the sentences as they follow one another, the music of the words, and the awful solemnity of thought and feeling which pervade this lofty utterance of faith and aspiration.

To have heard the writer of that prayer offering it up himself must have been an event in any man's life. I do not believe that any mere reading it *with the eye* could suffice to convey its mysterious power and significance, any more than the reading the score of one of Beethoven's symphonies could reveal the profounder messages which the great master's inspiration is meant to convey to the inner man.

The sermon itself can only be described as magnificent. The pathos of the occasion, the affectionate gratitude of the preacher, the sense of loss and bereavement, the love that he bore towards those that grieved, the memories of the long years that were the treasures of the past, and the faith and hope which claimed the great joy of the future,—if all these would not lift up the poet preacher to a supreme effort of something like inspired eloquence, would he have been what he was? The sermon was at once

13

called for, and was immediately published in a little
12mo volume. It is one of the rarest of books.
Happily, it has been reprinted more than once, and
there is a copy of it in its original form in the library
of the British Museum.

Within a few days of the death of Lady Danvers,
Donne lost another of those generous and devoted
friends who had stood by him so nobly in the years of
difficulty and anxiety when he was vainly looking out
for some post at court. Lucy, Countess of Bedford,
who had been living in retirement at Moor Park in
Hertfordshire, and there ministering tenderly at the
side of her much-afflicted husband, died on the 31st
of May, having survived the earl just three weeks.
She had been a great sufferer from a complication of
disorders for some years past. The old brilliant gaiety
had faded, the old beauty had passed, but faith and
trust had not left her, though she had almost become
forgotten by the world in which she had once been so
conspicuous a figure. About this time, too, Sir Henry
Goodere died. He had fallen into poverty, none the less
distressing because he had spent his fortune improvi-
dently, and had never received a post at court in
return for all his attendance at the old plays and
pageants; but I have no doubt that it was to him that
Izaak Walton refers when he says that Donne had
the happiness of being able in his later years to help
with the gift of £100 one special friend of his, " whom
he had known live plentifully, and by a too liberal
heart and carelessness became decayed in his estate."

There were other matters which contributed to
make this year a sad and anxious one for Donne. His
eldest son, John, whom he never names in his letters,

had already entered upon that course of dissipation and profligacy which in his later years made his name a reproach to all that bore it; and this very year he had, there is some reason to believe, made a disreputable marriage. His son George had taken to a military life; of his career we know little but that he was one of those taken prisoner at the disastrous retreat from the Isle of Rhé, and had already attained the rank of captain. His father was anxious about him, and had received no letters from him.

George Donne was kept in a French prison for five years—his father never saw him again. He procured his liberty in 1633, by bribing his jailer, and escaped safely to England.

During this year, too, his aged mother had become dependent upon her son by the death of her third (?) husband (Rainsford). Disregarding the ill-natured remarks which some made at the scandal of so noted a supporter of the Romanist faction being received into the deanery, Donne offered her there an asylum in her old age. She continued to live with her illustrious son till his death, and survived him nine months. She was buried at All Hallows, Barking, on the 28th January 1631[–2].

CHAPTER IX

LIFE'S EVENING AND THE SUNSET

IT was Donne's practice to keep the Festival of the Conversion of St. Paul by preaching in the Cathedral pulpit either upon the 25th January itself or upon the Sunday following. In the year 1628 he did so on Sunday the 27th, and thus began the new year. Three times during that spring he was called upon to preach before the king at Whitehall, and on Whit Sunday, as usual, he took his turn at St. Paul's. Shortly afterwards he left London to pay a visit to his parishioners at Sevenoaks, and during his absence his daughter Margaret was taken with the small-pox. The girl's attack was a mild one. She was carefully attended by an old servant, named Eliza-beth, who for many years had been the faithful "waiting-maid" and friend of herself and her sisters.[1] There was nothing to be gained by her father's re-maining to watch by her sickbed, and in the month of August he went down to Blunham, where he stayed for three weeks. On his way back to London he was seized with a fever "which," as he writes, "when Dr. Fox, whom I found at London, considered well and perceived the fever to be complicated with a squin-ancie [quinsy], by way of prevention of both he pre-

[1] Donne left a legacy of £20 to this good woman in his will.

196

sently took blood; and so with ten days starving in a close prison, that is, my bed, I am—blessed be God —returned to a convenient temper and pulse and appetite."

The symptoms appear to have been violent, and his "mouth and voice"—presumably his throat—were so affected that, he adds, "It is likely to take me from any frequent exercise of my duty of preaching. But God will either enable me or pardon me. His will be done upon us all."

A man of fifty-five finds it hard to believe that he has passed his prime and that he can no longer do as much and as well as he has been accustomed to do. In Donne's case, however, he had been living for years at very great tension, not only of mind but much more so of body, and his frequent and enthusiastic preaching had put so great a strain upon his constitution that his health was seriously breaking. The very last thing that he would have assented to was that a period of absolute rest had now become imperatively necessary; this was now forced upon him, much against his will, and for more than six months he was compelled to retire from all active work, insomuch that towards the end of the year a report was widely circulated that he was dead. He refers to this rumour in the following letter to Mrs. Cokayne:—

"I have found this rumour of my death to have made so deep impression and to have been so peremptorily believed, that from very remote parts I have been entreated to signify under my hand that I am yet alive. . . . What gave the occasion of this rumour I can make no conjecture. And yet the hour of my death and the day of my burial were related in the highest place of this kingdom. I had at that time no kind of sickness, nor was otherwise than I had been ever since my fever, and am yet: that is, too weak at this time of year to go forth especially to London . . . where I must necessarily open myself to more business than my present state could bear. Yet next term, by God's grace, I will be there."

He was better than his word; for he preached at St. Paul's on Christmas Day, taking as his text the words, "*Who hath believed our report ?* "—possibly with a latent allusion to the rumours that had been circulated regarding himself.

Next year, 1629, during the spring, he preached four or five times, at court and at St. Paul's; but in May he broke down again. In November he was so far recovered as to preach at Paul's Cross on Matt. xi. 6, and we may infer that a great crowd had assembled to hear him, from the following passage:—

" Beloved, there are poor that are *literally* poor, poor in estate and fortune; and poor, that are *naturally* poor, poor in capacity and understanding; and poor that are *spiritually* poor, dejected in spirit, and insensible of the comforts which the Holy Ghost offers unto them; and to all these poor, are we all bound to preach the gospel. . . . For them which are *literally* poor, poor in estate, how much do they want of this means of salvation—preaching—which the rich have ? They cannot maintain chaplains in their houses; they cannot forbear the necessary labours of their calling, to hear extraordinary sermons; *they cannot have seats in church whensoever they come ; they must stay, they must stand, they must thrust*, they must overcome

that difficulty, which St. Augustine makes an impossibility, that is for any man to receive benefit by
that sermon that he hears with pain: they must take
pains to hear. *To these poor, therefore, the Lord and
His Spirit* hath sent me to preach the gospel. . . . "

The sermon must have taken more than an hour to
deliver; it is singularly free from those quotations
from and references to other men's works and opinions
which sometimes weary us in the more laboured
efforts of the great preacher. Donne gives us here
more of himself, and surrenders himself to the impulse
of his own genius, or perhaps it would be truer to
say, he surrenders himself to the thoughts that had
been the subjects of his contemplation during the
past months, when his long illness had led him to
think of the nearness of death and of the beatific
vision that his soul desired. What is this blessedness
—he asks—which the Saviour speaks of in the text ?

" Blessedness itself is God Himself. Our blessedness
is our possession, our union with God. To see God
as He is, that is blessedness. There in heaven I
shall have *continuitatem intuendi* ; it is not only vision,
but intuition; not only a seeing, but a beholding, a
contemplating of God. . . . I shall be still but the
servant of my God, and yet I shall be of the same
spirit with that God. When ? . . . Our last day is
our first day ; our Saturday is our Sunday ; our eve
is our holy day ; our sunsetting is our morning ; the
day of our death is the first day of our eternal life.
The next day after that . . . comes that day that
shall show me to myself. Here I never saw myself
but in disguises ; there, then, I shall see myself, but I
shall see God too. . . . Here I have one faculty

enlightened, and another left in darkness ; mine understanding sometimes cleared, my will at the same time
perverted. There I shall be all light, no shadow
upon me; my soul invested in the light of joy, and
my body in the light of glory. . . . How glorious is
God as He calls up our eyes to Him in the beauty
and splendour and service of the Church! How
glorious in that spouse of His! But how glorious
shall I conceive this light to be when I shall see it
in His own place! In that sphere which, though a
sphere, is a centre too ; in that place which, though a
place, is all and everywhere!"

The preaching of this sermon overtaxed Donne's
failing strength ; for when Christmas Day came he was,
for the first time, unable to appear in the pulpit of
St. Paul's. He made amends for his absence then by
preaching one of his most ingenious and characteristic
sermons on the Feast of the Conversion of St. Paul
(25th January 1630). He chose as his text
Acts xxiii. 6, 7.

"In handling of which words," he says, ". . . we
shall stop *first* upon that consideration, that all the
actions of holy men . . . are not to be drawn into
example and consequence for others, no, nor always to be
excused and justified in them that did them. And
secondly we shall consider this action of St. Paul in
some circumstances that invest it. . . . And in a
third consideration we shall lodge all these in ourselves, and make it our own case, and find that we
have all Sadducees and Pharisees in our own bosoms
—contrary affections in our own hearts—and find
an advantage in putting these home - Sadducees
and home-Pharisees in colluctation and opposition

against one another. . . . A civil war is, in this case,
our way to peace:— . . .

"Paul's way was by a twofold protection; the first
this, *Men and brethren, I am a Pharisee!*

.   .   .   .

"Beloved, there are some things in which all religions
agree: the worship of God, the holiness of life.
Therefore, if (when I study this holiness of life, and
fast, and pray, and submit myself to discreet and
individual mortifications for the subduing of my body)
any man will say, 'This is papistical! Papists do
this!'—it is a blessed protestation, and no man is the
less a Protestant nor the worse a Protestant for making
it—'I am a Papist! that is, I will fast and pray as
much as any Papist, and enable myself for the service
of my God, as seriously, as sedulously, as laboriously
as any Papist.'

"So if—when I startle and am affected at the
blasphemous oath, as at a wound upon my Saviour—
if—when I avoid the conversation of those men that
profane the Lord's day—any other will say, 'This is
puritanical! Puritans do this!'—it is a blessed protestation, and no man is the less a Protestant nor the
worse a Protestant for making it—'Men and brethren,
I am a Puritan! that is, I will endeavour to be pure,
as my Father in heaven is pure—as far as any
Puritan!'

.   .   .   .

"End we all with this; we have all these Sadducees
and Pharisees in our own bosoms. . . . Sins of presumption and carnal confidence are our Sadducees; and
then our Pharisees are our sins of separation, of division,
of diffidence and distrust in the mercies of our God. . . .

Now if I go St. Paul's way, to put a dissension between these my Sadducees and my Pharisees, to put a jealousy between my presumption and my desperation, . . . I may, as St. Paul did in the text, 'scape the better for that. . . .

"That God that is the God of peace, grant us His peace and one mind one towards another. That God that is the Lord of hosts, maintain in us that war which Himself hath proclaimed ; an enmity between the seed of the woman and the seed of the serpent, between the truth of God and the inventions of men ; that we may fight His battles against His enemies without, and fight His battles against His enemies within—our own corrupt affections ; that we may be victorious here, in ourselves and over ourselves, and triumph with Him hereafter in eternal glory."

Donne preached his last sermon at St. Paul's on Easter Day, 28th March 1630. Then he broke down again.[1]

. . . . . .

It will be remembered that Donne's eldest daughter, Constance, had been married in December 1623 to Edward Allen. She was left a widow on 25th Nov. 1626. She was comfortably provided for, and continued a widow until the 24th June of this year 1630, when she married as her second husband Mr. Samuel Harvey of Aldborough Hatch, near Barking, in Essex. The newly-married pair had known each other all their lives ; for the husband was a grandson of Sir James Harvey, to whom the dean's father had

---

[1] The sermon said to have been preached "in Lent to the king, *April* 20, 1630 " (vol. i. folio, p. 127), is certainly wrongly dated. In that year the 3rd *Sunday after Easter* fell upon the 23rd April.

served his time before his admission to the freedom of the city of London ; and as prominent members of the Ironmongers' Company the two men must have been brought into close business relations with one another, till the early death of Donne's father brought these to a close.

Whether Donne was able to be present at this second marriage—which appears to have taken place from the house of her uncle, Sir Thomas Grymes, at Camberwell—we are not told ; but two months later Walton assures us that his friend went down to Abrey Hatch (as it was pronounced) to pay a visit to his daughter, and while with her "he fell into a fever," from the effects of which he never quite recovered.   By this time he had begun to realise that his earthly career was drawing to a close, and that there was little for him now to do save to make all needful preparations for the end that was at hand. Cut off as he was from the privilege of preaching during the winter of 1629, and now again during the greater part of 1630, he employed himself in preparing his sermons for the press, and in writing or expanding some of those with which he was not satisfied.   Thus, in a prefatory note to the two sermons on Matthew iv. 18, 20, he writes : "At the Hague, Dec. 19, 1619, I preached upon this text.   Since in sickness at Abrey Hatch in Essex, 1630, revising my short notes of that sermon, I digested them into these two."   In the three folios published by Donne's son between 1640 and 1660, there are five or six of these double sermons which internal evidence proves were never preached as they stand in the printed text ; and in a precious volume in my possession, prepared by Donne himself for the press, written throughout in his own hand, there is one long sermon (on Luke iii. 21, 22) left unfinished, but followed by eleven blank pages evidently meant to be written on, though the writer never carried out his intention. There is also what may be called a fantastic treatise upon *Jacob's Ladder* in the form of a sermon on Gen. xxviii. 12, 13, which could never have been delivered, or indeed intended to be delivered, inasmuch as it would take at least three hours to *read* aloud.

During all this long period of enforced idleness, so far from his intellect suffering any loss of power or from weariness, Walton assures us that "the latter part of his life may be said to have been a continual study."

As it had been in 1624, when in the very crisis of what threatened to be a fatal illness he went on writing diligently day by day even for hours at a time, so it was now: his mind was incessantly at work, and the extraordinary versatility of his genius showed itself in the many curious fancies that were the subjects of his thoughts. He had been heretofore wont to seal his letters with an impression of his family crest—*a knot of snakes* argent; during his last illness he seems to have discarded this signet, "and not long before his death he caused to be drawn a figure of the body of Christ extended upon an anchor, like those which painters draw when they would present us with the picture of Christ crucified on the cross: his varying no otherwise than to affix Him not to a cross, but to an anchor—the emblem of Hope; this he caused to be drawn in little, and then many of those figures thus drawn to be engraven very small

Corporis hæc Animæ sit Syndon Syndon Jesu
Amen.

Martin Dr scup. And are to be sould by R R and Ben ffisher

in heliotropium stones and set in gold; and of these he sent to many of his dearest friends, to be used as seals or rings, and kept as memorials of him and of his affection to them." Walton names five of these friends, George Herbert being one of them. He does not mention his own name, though the ring which Donne gave to honest Izaak Walton has been handed down as an heirloom in the family of his descendants.

It was about this time that Dr. Fox, the physician who was in constant attendance upon him during his last illness, suggested that a monument should be prepared for him, to be set up in St. Paul's after his death. "Dr. Donne, by the persuasion of Dr. Fox, easily yielded at this very time to have a monument made for him; but Dr. Fox undertook not to persuade him how, or what monument it should be; that was left to Dr. Donne himself.

" A monument being resolved upon, Dr. Donne sent for a carver to make for him in wood the figure of an urn, giving him directions for the compass and height of it; and to bring with it a board, of the just height of his body. These being got, then without delay a choice painter was got to be in readiness to draw his picture, which was taken as followeth :—Several charcoal fires being first made in his large study, he brought with him into that place his winding-sheet in his hand, and having put off all his clothes, had this sheet put on him, and so tied with knots at his head and feet, and his hands so placed, as dead bodies are usually fitted to be shrouded, and put into their coffin or grave. Upon this urn he thus stood, with his eyes shut, and with so much of the sheet turned aside as might show his lean, pale, and death-like face, which was purposely turned towards the east, from whence he expected the second coming of his and our Saviour Jesus. In this posture he was drawn at his just height; and when the picture was fully finished, he caused it to be set by his bedside, where it continued and became his hourly object till his death, and was then given to his dearest friend and executor, Dr. Henry King, then chief residentiary of St. Paul's, who caused him to be thus carved in one entire piece of white marble, as it now stands in that church." [1]

Though Donne seems to have considered himself bound by his half promise to Lady Bedford to write no more verse after he had been admitted to holy orders, yet by her ladyship's death he appears to have thought himself released from any such pledge, and now in his lonely hours he found a solace in surrendering himself to his poetic gift. How much of his religious poetry he wrote at this time it is impossible to conjecture; but the magnificent hymn which he calls "An Hymn to God the Father" must have been written at this period, though Walton suggests that it was composed at an earlier date. Familiar as it doubtless is to most of us, it would be unpardonable to omit it here.

"Wilt Thou forgive that sin where I begun,
   Which was my sin, though it were done before?
Wilt Thou forgive that sin through which I run,
   And do run still, though still I do deplore?
When Thou hast done, Thou hast not done,
              For I have more.

---

[1] This was one of the few monuments which escaped the ravages of the great fire in 1666, and has within the last few years been set up again in the south aisle of the choir.

Wilt Thou forgive that sin, which I have won
  Others to sin, and made my sin their door?
Wilt Thou forgive that sin which I did shun
  A year or two—but wallowed in a score?
When Thou hast done, Thou hast not done,
                For I have more.

I have a sin of fear that when I've spun
  My last thread, I shall perish on the shore;
But swear by Thyself, that at my death Thy Son
  Shall shine as He shines now, and heretofore;
And having done that, Thou hast done,
              I fear no more."

" I have," writes Walton, " the rather mentioned this
hymn, for that he caused it to be set to a most grave
and solemn tune, and to be often sung to the organ
by the choristers of St. Paul's Church, in his own
hearing, especially at the evening service; and at his
return from his customary devotions in that place,
did occasionally say to a friend, ' The words of this
hymn have restored to me the same thoughts of joy
that possessed my soul in my sickness, when I composed it. And, O the power of church music! that
harmony added to this hymn has raised the affections
of my heart and quickened my graces of zeal and
gratitude; and I observe that I always return from
paying this public duty of prayer and praise to God,
with an unexpressible tranquillity of mind, and a
willingness to leave the world.' "

During these last years of his life Donne continued
writing sedulously to [his old friends; and of these
letters several have come down to us which afford
us a pathetic insight into his thoughts and occupations
as the days passed on. He was anxious and a little
troubled about his son George, who was still in a

French prison. Some great lady had borrowed a sum of money from him and left her diamonds with him as a security for the loan. Donne, in view of his approaching end, was uneasy at the thought that the jewels might be found in the deanery after his death, and a scandal might be occasioned or difficulties arise; and he writes to his old friend, George Garrard, who was at this time Master of Charterhouse, begging him in some way to relieve him of the embarrassment of the situation.

The saddest letter is a long one addressed to Mrs. Cokayne, who had made a somewhat peremptory application for a living in the dean's gift which had just fallen vacant. Mrs. Cokayne was exceedingly anxious to get it for a certain Nathaniel Hazard, of whom nothing is known except that he had been a tutor in Mrs. Cokayne's family. Donne's letter in reply will tell its own tale :—

"My NOBLE SISTER,—I am afraid that Death will play with me so long as he will forget to kill me; and suffer me to live in a languishing and useless age a life that is rather a forgetting that I am dead than of living. We dispute whether the dead shall pray for the living, and because my life may be short, I pray with the most earnestness for you now. By the advantage of sickness, I return the oftener to that holy exercise, and in it join yours with mine own soul. I would not have dignified myself or my sickness with saying so much of either, but that it is in obedience to your command that I should do so. And though there lie upon me no command, yet there lies a necessity growing out of my respect and a

nobler root than that, my love to you, to enlarge
myself, as far as I have gone already in this Mr.
Hazard's business. My noble sister, when you carry
me up to the beginning, which it pleases you to call
a promise to yourself, and your noble sister; I never
slackened my purpose of performing that promise.
But if my promise, which was that I should be ready
to assist him in any thing I could, were translated by
you, or your noble sister or him, that I would give
him the next living in my gift, certainly we speak
not one language, or understand not one another, and
I had thought we had. This which he imagined to
be vacant (for it is not yet nor any way likely) is the
first that fell to me since I made that promise. And,
my noble sister: if a person of my place from whom
one scholar in each university sucks something and
must be weaned by me, and who hath otherwise a
latitude of unfortunate friends and very many obligations, hast a living once in five or six years fall in
his gift (for it is so long since I gave any), and may
not make a good choice with freedom then, it is hard;
yet it is not my fortune to do so now: for, now there
is a living fallen (though not that), I am not left to
my choice, for my Lord Carlisle and Percy have
chosen for me : but truly such a man as I would have
chosen : and for him, they laid an obligation upon me
three years since, for the next that should fall; yet
Mr. Hazard presses you to write for that, because he
to whom my promise belongs hath another before,
but doth he or his lord owe me any thing for that ?
Yet Mr. Hazard importunes me, to press that chaplain
of my lord, that when he takes mine, he shall resign
the other to him, which, as it is an ignorant request

14

(for if it be resign'd it is not in his power to place it
upon Mr. Hazard), so it is an unjust request that I
that give him fifty pounds a year should take from
him forty. But amongst Mr. Hazard's manifold
importunities that that I took worst was that he
should write of domestic things, and what I said of
my son, to you : and arm you with that plea that my
son was not in orders. But, my noble sister, though I
am far from drawing my son immaturely into orders,
or putting into his hands any church with cure : yet
there are many prebends and other helps in the
church, which a man without taking orders may be
capable of, and for some such I might change a living
with cure, and so begin to accommodate a son in some
preparation. But Mr. Hazard is too piercing. It is
good counsel (and as I remember I gave it him) that
if a man deny him any thing and accompany his
denial with a reason, he be not too searching whether
that be the true reason or no, but rest in the denial :
for many times it may be out of my power to do a
man a courtesy which he desires and yet I not tied
to tell him the true reason : therefore out of his letter
to you, I continue my opinion that he meddled too
far herein. I cannot shut my letter till (whilst we are
upon this consideration of reasons of denials) I tell
you one answer of his, which perchance may weaken
your so great assurance of his modesty. I told him
that my often sicknesses had brought me to an inability
of preaching, and that I was under a necessity of
preaching twelve or fourteen solemn sermons every
year, to great auditories, at Paul's, and to the Judges,
and at courts, and that therefore I must think of
conferring something upon such a man as may supply

my place in these solemnities, and surely, said I, I
will offer them no man in those cases which shall not
be at least equal to myself; and, Mr. Hazard, I do
not know your faculties. He gave me this answer.
' I will not make comparisons, but I do not doubt but
that I should give them satisfaction in that kind.'
Now, my noble sister, whereas you repeat often, that
you and your sister rested upon my word and my
worth, and but for my word and my worth you would
not have proceeded so far : I must necessarily make
my protestation, that my word and my worth is,
herein, chaste and untouched. For, my noble sister,
goes there no more to the giving of a scholar a church
in London but that he was a young gentleman school-
master ? You know the ticklishness of London
pulpits, and how ill it would become me, to place a
man in a London church that were not both a strong
and a sound man. And therefore those things must
come into consideration before he can have a living
from me though there was no need of reflecting upon
those things when I made that general promise, that
I would assist his fortune in any thing. You end in
a phrase of indignation and displeasure rare in you
towards me, therefore it affects me : which is, that he
may part from me as I received him at first ; as though
I were likely to hinder him. The heat that produced
that word I know is past, and therefore, my most
beloved sister, give me leave to say to you that he
shall not part from me, but I shall keep him still in
my care, and make you always my judge of all omissions.

" Your faithful friend and servant."

Mrs. Cokayne took this remonstrance in the spirit

in which it was written, and the affectionate letter
which Donne wrote to her a few days before he left
Abrey Hatch, to return thanks, shows that the understanding between the two friends continued then to
be as cordial as ever; and this is the last letter that
has come down to us.

Donne made his will at his daughter's house on the
13th December 1630. Weak and frail as he was, he
could not yet give up the hope of being able to preach
once more at St. Paul's on Christmas Day. When he
was persuaded that this was impossible, he still hoped
to be at his post on Candlemas Day (2nd February),
but again he had to find a substitute.

"Before that month ended, he was appointed to
preach upon his old constant day, the first Friday in
Lent: he had notice of it, and had in his sickness so
prepared for that employment, that as he had long
thirsted for it, so he resolved his weakness should not
hinder his journey; he came therefore to London some
few days before his appointed day of preaching. At
his coming thither, many of his friends—who with
sorrow saw his sickness had left him but so much
flesh as did only cover his bones—doubted his strength
to perform that task, and did therefore dissuade him
from undertaking it, assuring him, however, it was
like to shorten his life: but he passionately denied
their requests, saying, 'He would not doubt that that
God, who in so many weaknesses had assisted him
with an unexpected strength, would now withdraw it
in his last employment; professing a holy ambition to
perform that sacred work.' And when, to the amaze-
ment of some beholders, he appeared in the pulpit,
many of them thought he presented himself not to

preach mortification by a living voice, but mortality
by a decayed body and a dying face.   And doubtless
many did secretly ask that question in Ezekiel (chap.
xxxvii. 3), 'Do these bones live? or can that soul
organise that tongue to speak so long time as the
sand in that glass will move towards its centre, and
measure out an hour of this dying man's unspent life?
Doubtless it cannot.'   And yet, after some faint
pauses in his zealous prayer, his strong desires enabled
his weak body to discharge his memory of his precon-
ceived meditations, which were of dying; the text
being, 'To God the Lord belong the issues from
death.'   Many that then saw his tears, and heard his
faint and hollow voice, professing they thought the
text prophetically chosen, and that Dr. Donne had
preached his own funeral sermon.

" Being full of joy that God had enabled him to
perform this desired duty, he hastened to his house;
out of which he never moved, till, like St. Stephen,
' he was carried by devout men 'to his grave.' [1]

" The next day after his sermon, his strength being
much wasted, and his spirits so spent as indisposed
him to business or to talk, a friend that had often
been a witness of his free and facetious discourse
asked him, ' Why are you sad?'   To whom he
replied, with a countenance so full of cheerful gravity,
as gave testimony of an inward tranquillity of mind,
and of a soul willing to take a farewell of this world;
and said: .

" ' I am not sad; but most of the night past I have

---

[1] The Gregorian Calendar was not accepted at this time in England.
Therefore, according to our reckoning, the 1st Friday in Lent fell on
the 25th February.   Donne died on the 31st March.

entertained myself with many thoughts of several
friends that have left me here, and are gone to that
place from which they shall not return; and that
within a few days I also shall go hence, and be no
more seen. And my preparation for this change has
become my nightly meditation upon my bed, which
my infirmities have now made restless to me. But at
this present time, I was in a serious contemplation of
the providence and goodness of God to me; to me,
who am less than the least of His mercies: and looking back upon my life past, I now plainly see it was
His hand that prevented me from all temporal
employment; and that it was His will I should never
settle nor thrive till I entered into the Ministry, in
which I have now lived almost twenty years—I hope
to His glory—and by which, I most humbly thank
Him, I have been enabled to requite most of those
friends which showed me kindness when my fortune
was very low, as God knows it was: and—as it hath
occasioned the expression of my gratitude—I thank
God most of them have stood in need of my requital.
I have lived to be useful and comfortable to my good
father-in-law, Sir George More, whose patience God
hath been pleased to exercise with many temporal
crosses; I have maintained my own mother, whom it
hath pleased God, after a plentiful fortune in her
younger days, to bring to great decay in her very old
age. I have quieted the consciences of many that
have groaned under the burthen of a wounded spirit,
whose prayers I hope are available for me. I cannot
plead innocency of life, especially of my youth; but I
am to be judged by a merciful God, who is not willing
to see what I have done amiss. And though of my-

self I have nothing to present to Him but sins and misery, yet I know He looks not upon me now as I am of myself, but as I am in my Saviour, and hath given me, even at this present time, some testimonies by His Holy Spirit, that I am of the number of His Elect: I am therefore full of inexpressible joy, and shall die in peace.' "

There was no more work remaining to be done. The sands of life were fast running out. Eight days before the end came he wrote his last poem on his deathbed, which bore the title—

"An Hymn to God, my God, in my Sickness." March 23, 1630.

The first and last verses are those best worth quoting :—

> "Since I am coming to that holy room,
>   Where, with Thy Choir of Saints, for evermore
> I shall be made Thy music, as I come
>   I tune my instrument here at the door,
>   And, what I must do then, think here before.
>
>   .   .   .   .
>
> So, in His purple wrapt, receive me, Lord !
>   By these His thorns, give me His other Crown :
> And, as to other souls I preached Thy word,
>   Be this my text, my sermon to mine own,
>   'Therefore, that He may raise, the Lord throws down.'"

He had only three days to live when he became disturbed by anxiety regarding the large mass of manuscripts which he was about to leave behind him. By some strange misadventure he had made no mention of these in his will; and inasmuch as they not only comprehended an immense accumulation of miscellaneous notes and extracts, the *Ephemerides* of a student of extraordinary industry during nearly fifty years of research, but also included all his sermons and other writings, representing in the aggregate a collection which even in those days was worth no inconsiderable sum of money, common prudence would have suggested that this literary property should be dealt with by a special bequest. Donne had and could have no confidence in his son John, and in view of what might happen he endeavoured to provide against a contingency which actually did happen. So far as at this stage it was possible for him to do so without adding a codicil to his will, he endeavoured to make a surrender of his manuscripts by deed of gift to Dr. King, one of his executors. Among them were the sermons prepared for the press and afterwards published in folio, "together with which," says Dr. King himself—"as his best legacy—he gave me all his sermon notes and his other papers, containing an extract of near fifteen hundred, professing before Dr. Winniff, Dr. Montford [and Izaak Walton], then present at his bedside, that it was my restless importunity that he had prepared them for the press."

Unhappily, very soon after Donne's death, and while the estate was in the custody of the executors, his son John, as heir-male, laid claim to the whole of these literary remains; and Dr. King was—under pressure the nature of which remains unexplained—compelled to surrender them.

Thirty years later, in a letter to Izaak Walton, King, complaining of this outrage, writes: "How these were got out of my hands, you who were the messenger for them, and how lost to me and yourself, is not now seasonable to complain." The collection appears to have been kept in the first instance in a cabinet reserved for it—an illustration this of the dean's methodical habits which Walton remarks upon. It looks as if towards the close of his life the younger Donne felt some compunction or shame at the wrong he had done to his father and his father's friend; for in his will, which he drew up in 1662, he says, "To the Reverent Bishop of Chichester I return the *cabinet* that was my father's, now in my dining-room, and all those papers which are of authors analysed by my father; *many* of which he hath already received with *his Common Place Book*, which I desire may pass to Mr. Walton's son as being most likely to have use for such a help when his age shall require it."

Many attempts have been made to discover what became of these papers, but without result. It is evident they were practically kept together till some years after the Restoration, but in Bishop King's will, subscribed by him 14th July 1663, and proved *without any* codicils in 1669, there is no mention of or allusion to the Donne MSS., nor does the name of Izaak Walton the younger occur.

.   .   .   .

"Thus variable, thus virtuous was the life; thus excellent, thus exemplary was the death of this memorable man."

So writes Izaak Walton, as he prepares to add the last few sentences to that masterpiece of English biography which he entitles the *Life of Dr. John Donne.* It is no panegyric; it is much less a mere dry recital of facts. If, as some tell us, poetry is the language of excited feeling, never was there a more truly poetic story written than Walton's life of Donne.

It is a story told in solemn rhythmic prose, throbbing
with a burden of tender memories and fond regrets
too full of blessed associations to allow of any gloom
in recording them. It is an idealised picture of his
master, *famous, calm and dead,* drawn by a disciple
who had loved that master with enthusiastic loyalty
and reverence, loved him " on this side idolatry."
Walton could afford to be careless about details
and accessories when he was setting down the re-
miniscences of others regarding Donne's early life.
It seems he could only have known him intimately for
the five or six years before he died. They were long
enough, however, to draw together by the mysterious
attractive force of sympathy the two men of genius
who in the circumstances of their lives and their
education had so little in common. Once brought
together in close relations, and a subtile affinity
between the two united them more and more closely
from day to day. While Donne lay dying, Walton
was always at his side—he seems never to have left
him. We have no such grand and pathetic narrative
of the passing of a dying saint of God.

It was not till the 31st March 1631 that the
gracious summons came.

Let Izaak Walton draw the curtain. It would be
little less than profanation to substitute for his closing
words of this life's drama any others that we of the
common herd could write down.

" The Sunday following he appointed his servants
that, if there were any business yet undone that
concerned him or themselves, it should be prepared
against Saturday next, for after that day he would
not mix his thoughts with anything that concerned

this world, nor ever did; but as Job, so he 'waited for the appointed day of his dissolution.'

" And now he was so happy as to have nothing to do but to die, to do which he stood in need of no longer time; for he had studied it long, and to so happy a perfection, that in a former sickness he called God to witness (in his 'Book of Devotions,' written then), 'He was that minute ready to deliver his soul into His hands, if that minute God would determine his dissolution.' In that sickness he begged of God the constancy to be preserved in that estate for ever; and his patient expectation to have his immortal soul disrobed from her garment of mortality, makes me confident that he now had a modest assurance that his prayers were then heard and his petition granted. He lay fifteen days earnestly expecting his hourly change; and in the last hour of his last day, as his body melted away, and vapoured into spirit, his soul having, I verily believe, some revelation of the beatifical vision, he said, 'I were miserable if I might not die;' and after those words, closed many periods of his faint breath by saying often, 'Thy kingdom come, Thy will be done.' His speech, which had long been his ready and faithful servant, left him not till the last minute of his life, and then forsook him, not to serve another master—for who speaks like him—but died before him; for that it was then become useless to him that now conversed with God on earth as angels are said to do in heaven, only by thoughts and looks. Being speechless, and seeing heaven by that illumination by which he saw it, he did, as St. Stephen, ' look steadfastly into it, till he saw the Son of Man standing at the right hand of

God His Father,' and being satisfied with this blessed
sight, as his soul ascended and his last breath departed from him, he closed his own eyes, and then
disposed his hands and body into such a posture as
required not the least alteration by those that came
to shroud him.

"He was buried in that place of St. Paul's Church
which he had appointed for that use some years
before his death, and by which he passed daily to
pay his public devotions to Almighty God, who was
then served twice a day by a public form of prayer
and praises in that place; but he was not buried
privately, though he desired it, for, beside an un-
numbered number of others, many persons of nobility
and of eminence for learning, who did love and
honour him in his life, did show it at his death, by
a voluntary and sad attendance of his body to the
grave, where nothing was so remarkable as a public
sorrow.

"To which place of his burial some mournful friends
repaired, and, as Alexander the Great did to the
grave of the famous Achilles, so they strewed his with
an abundance of curious and costly flowers, which
course they, who were never yet known, continued
morning and evening for many days, not ceasing till
the stones that were taken up in that church to give
his body admission into the cold earth—now his
bed of rest—were again by the mason's art so
levelled and firmed as they had been formerly, and
his place of burial undistinguishable to common
view.

"The next day after his burial some unknown friend,
some one of the many lovers and admirers of his

virtue and learning, writ this epitaph with a coal on
the wall over his grave:—

'Reader! I am to let thee know,
Donne's body only lies below;
For, could the grave his soul comprise,
Earth would be richer than the skies!'

"Nor was this all the honour done to his reverend
ashes; for, as there be some persons that will not
receive a reward for that for which God accounts
Himself a debtor, persons that dare trust God with
their charity, and without a witness, so there was by
some grateful unknown friend that thought Dr.
Donne's memory ought to be perpetuated, a hundred
marks sent to his faithful friends and executors (Dr.
King and Dr. Montford), towards the making of his
monument. It was not for many years known by
whom; but, after the death of Dr. Fox, it was known
that it was he that sent it, and he lived to see as
lively a representation of his dead friend as marble
can express; a statue indeed so like Dr. Donne, that
—as his friend Sir Henry Wotton hath expressed
himself—'It seems to breathe faintly, and posterity
shall look upon it as a kind of artificial miracle.'

"He was of stature moderately tall, of a straight and
equally proportioned body, to which all his words and
actions gave an unexpressible addition of comeliness.

"The melancholy and pleasant humour were in him
so contempered that each gave advantage to the
other, and made his company one of the delights of
mankind.

"His fancy was unimitably high, equalled only by
his great wit, both being made useful by a commanding judgment.

" His aspect was cheerful, and such as gave a silent testimony of a clear knowing soul, and of a conscience at peace with itself.

" His melting eye showed that he had a soft heart, full of noble compassion ; of too brave a soul to offer injuries, and too much a Christian not to pardon them in others.

" He did much contemplate, especially after he entered into his sacred calling, the mercies of Almighty God, the immortality of the soul, and the joys of heaven, and would often say in a kind of sacred ecstasy, ' Blessed be God that He is God, only and divinely like Himself.'

" He was by nature highly passionate, but more apt to reluct at the excesses of it. A great lover of the offices of humanity, and of so merciful a spirit that he never beheld the miseries of mankind without pity and relief.

" He was earnest and unwearied in the search of knowledge, with which his vigorous soul is now satisfied, and employed in a continual praise of that God that first breathed it into his active body, that body which once was a temple of the Holy Ghost, and is now become a small quantity of Christian dust.

"BUT I SHALL SEE IT REANIMATED!"

APPENDIX A

PEDIGREE SHOWING THE DESCENT OF DOCTOR DONNE FROM ELIZABETH, SISTER OF SIR THOMAS MORE, THE LORD CHANCELLOR, EXECUTED IN 1536.

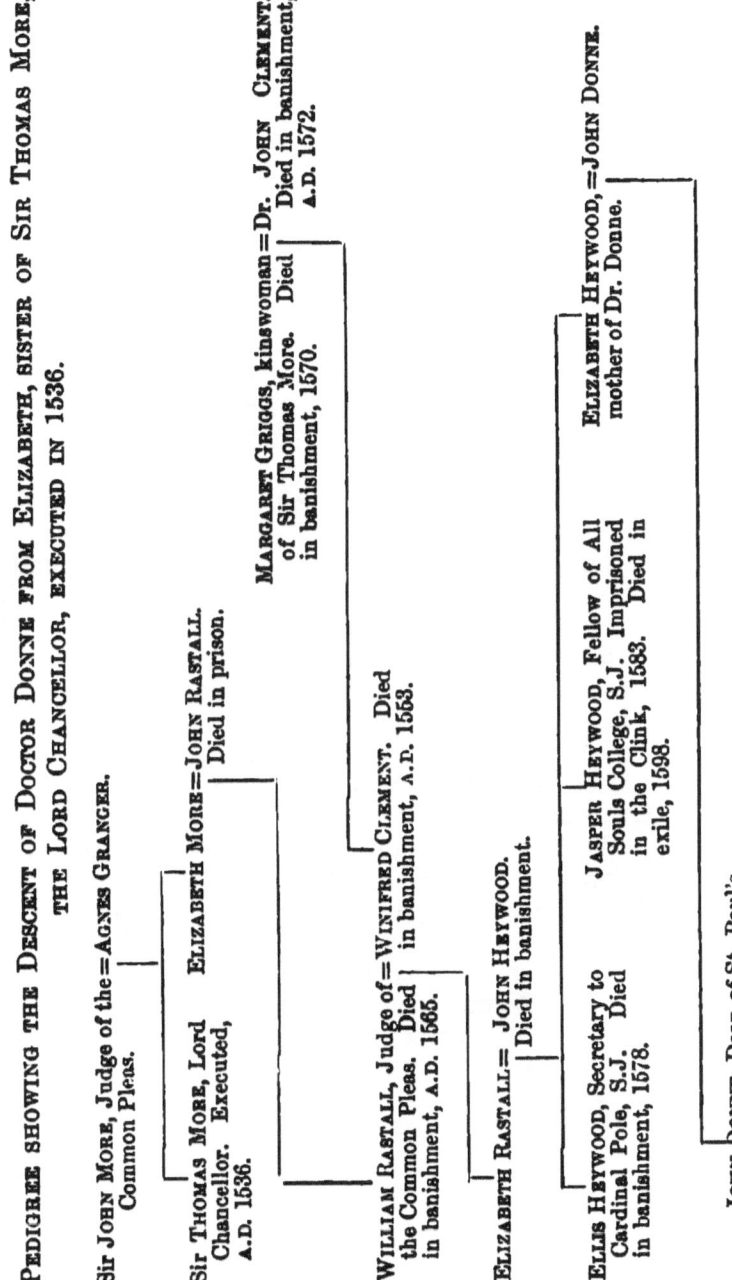

Sir John More, Judge of the = Agnes Granger.
Common Pleas.

Sir Thomas More, Lord Chancellor. Executed, A.D. 1536.

Elizabeth More = John Rastall.
Died in prison.

Margaret Griggs, kinswoman = Dr. John Clement.
of Sir Thomas More. Died Died in banishment,
in banishment, 1570. A.D. 1572.

William Rastall, Judge of = Winifred Clement. Died
the Common Pleas. Died in banishment, A.D. 1563.
in banishment, A.D. 1565.

Elizabeth Rastall = John Heywood.
Died in banishment.

Jasper Heywood, Fellow of All
Souls College, S.J. Imprisoned
in the Clink, 1583. Died in
exile, 1598.

Elizabeth Heywood, = John Donne.
mother of Dr. Donne.

Ellis Heywood, Secretary to
Cardinal Pole, S.J. Died
in banishment, 1578.

John Donne, Dean of St. Paul's.

APPENDIX B

DR. DONNE'S CHILDREN

IN the monumental inscription which Donne set up in the
old Church of St. Clement Danes, in memory of his wife,
he states that she died on the 15th August 1617.—*Vii. post
xii. partum (quorum vii. supersunt) dies.*

Whatever may be meant by the expression "*xii. partum,*"
it is clear that at her death Mrs. Donne left seven children
behind her. Of each and all of them we can give some
account.

1. CONSTANCE has been usually assumed to have been
   Donne's eldest child. She was probably born at
   Pyrford in 1603. She married, first, Edward Allen
   in 1623, and, secondly, Samuel Harvey in 1630. By
   her first husband she had no offspring; by her second
   she had at least three sons, whose names, but their
   names only, we know.

2. JOHN.—Of him a sufficient account will be found in
   the *Dictionary of National Biography.* He, too,
   was probably born at Pyrford in 1604. He married
   Mary Staples, of whom nothing is known, at Camberwell, 27th March 1627. There seems to have
   been no issue of the marriage. She seems to have
   died early, as no mention is made of either mother
   or child in the wills of Dr. Donne or of his son.

3. GEORGE.—He was baptized at Camberwell, 9th May
   1605. He was a prisoner of war in France at the
   time of his father's death, but returned to England
   in 1633 or 1634, and appears to have married some
   time after, for the baptism of a daughter of his is
   entered in the Register of Camberwell, 22nd March
   1638. Nothing more is known of him.

4. Lucy.—Baptized at Micham, 8th January 1608, Lady Bedford standing as her gódmother. She died unmarried, and was buried at Camberwell, 9th June 1626.

5. Bridget.—Unmarried, but "of years to govern herself," when her father made his will; was probably born between 1609 and 1612. She became the wife of Thomas Gardiner, Esq., of Peckham, son of Sir Thomas Gardiner of Camberwell (Blanch, *History of the Parish of Cumberwell*). Nothing further is known of her.

6. Margaret.—Some years after her father's death married Sir William Bowles of Clerkenwell. Eventually she died at Chislehurst in Kent, and was buried in the church-porch there. She had at least one daughter.

7. Elizabeth.—On the 18th May 1637 married Cornelius Lawrence, Doctor of Physic, at All Hallows, Barking.

The last two children were evidently young girls in 1630.

It is clear from the above, that at the time of Donne's death only two of his children were married. Constance had at that time no family; and there is a strong presumption that the wife of his son John was then dead, and died childless.

My belief is that neither of Donne's sons had any male offspring. It is hardly conceivable, that if at the end of the seventeenth century any descendants of the Dean entitled to perpetuate his illustrious name had been still living, the fact should have remained undiscovered down to our own time.

APPENDIX C

DONNE'S WILL

In the name of the holy blessed and glorious Trinitie Amen.

I JOHN DONNE by the Mercye of Christe Jesus and by the callinge of the Churche of Englande Preist beinge at this tyme in good & perfect understandinge praysed be God therefore, doe hereby make my last Will and Testament in manner and forme followinge.

Firste I give my good and gracious God an intire Sacrifice of body & soule wth my moste humble thanks for that assurance wch his blessed Spiritt ymprints in me nowe of the Salvation of the one & the Resurrection of the other and for that constant & cheerful resolucon wch the same Spiritte established in me to live & dye in the Religion nowe professed in the Churche of Englande   In expectation of that Resurrection I desyre that my body may be buryed in the moste private manner that maye be in that place of S^{nt}. Paules Churche London wch the nowe Residentiaries of that Church have bene pleased at my requeste to assigne for that purpose.

Item I make my well beloved friends *Henrye Kinge* Doctor of Divinitie & *John Montford* Doctor of Divinitie bothe Residentiaries of the Churche of S^{nt}. Pauls London Executors of this my Will.

And my will & desyre is that my verie worthie friend and Kynde Brother in Lawe Sr *Thomas Grymes* of Peckham in the Countye of Surrye Knighte be Overseer of this my Will To whom I give hereby that strykinge clocke wch I ordinarilye weare and alsoe the Picture of Kinge James.

To *Dcor Kinge* my Executor I give that Medall of Gold of the Synod of Dort which the Estates presented me w^{thall} at the Hague as also the twoe Pictures of Padre Paolo and Fulgentio wch hange in the Parlo^r. at my house at Pauls and to *Doctor Montford* my other Executor I give forty ounces of white plate and the twoe pictures that hange on the same syde of the Parlo^r.

Item I give to the Righte Hono^rable the *Earle of Carlisle* the Picture of the Blessed Virgin Marye wch hangs in the little Dynynge Chamber. And to the Right Hono^rable the *Earle of Dorse^lt.* the Picture of Adam and Eve W^ch hangs in the greate chamber.

Item I give to *Doctor Winniffe* Deane of Glocester and Residentiarie of S^t. Pauls the Picture called the Sceleton wch hangs in the Hall and to my kynde frend M^r. *George Garrard* the Picture of Marye Magdalene in my Chamber and to my ancient frend *Dẽor Brooke* Master of Trinitie College in Cambridge the Picture of the B. Virgin and Joseph wch. hangs in my Studey and to M^r. *Tourvall* a French Minister (but by the Ordination of the Englishe Churche) I give any Picture wch. he will chuse of those W^ch. hange in the little Dynynge roome & are not formerley bequeathed.

Item I give to my two faithfull servants *Robert Christmass* and *Thomas Roper* officers of the Churche of S^t. Paul's to eache of them Five pounds to make them seale ringes engraved wth. that Figure wch. I usuallye seale w^thall. of wch. sorte they knowe I have given many to my particular frendes.

Item I give to my God Daughter *Constance Grymes* Tenn pounds to be bestowed in plate for her.

Item I give to that Mayde whoe hathe many yeares attended my Daughters whose name is *Elizabeth,* Twenty pounds if shee shall be in my se^rvice at the tyme of my deathe and to the other mayde servants wch shall be in my service at that tyme I give a yeares wages over and beyond that wch shall at that time be due to them.

Item I give to *Vincent* my coachman and to my servant *John Christmass* to eache of them Ten pounds if they be at the tyme of my deathe in my service.

Item I give to *Thomas Moore* a younge boy whome I tooke latelie Five pounds if he shal be in my service then and if any of these servants shall be departed from me before I give to everie man servant that shall at that tyme be in my service a yeares wages over & above that wch shall be then due to them.

Item I give to each of the petty canons and vicars chorall wch shall be in the Churche of S^t. Paule at the tyme of my deathe To each of them Fortye shillings and Fortye shillings to the M^r. of the Choristers and Fortye shillings to be equally distributed amongst the then Choristers.

Item I give Thirtye shillings to eache of the vergers and to each of the bell ringers Twentye shillings.

Item I will and bequeath to my Cosyn *Jane Kent* who hathe heretofore been servant to my mother Twelve pounds and to my Cosyn *Edward Dawson* being decayed Twelve pounds and to his Sister *Grace Dawson* Six pounds wch proporčon they being aged persons I make accounte dothe annswere those penčons wch I have yearlie heretofore given unto them and meant to have contynued for theire lives if it had pleased to God to have contynued myne.

Item my will is that the fower large pictures of the fower greate Prophetts wch hange in the Hall and that large picture of ancient church work wch hange in the Lobby leadinge to my chamber And whatsov^r. I have placd in the Chappell (excepted that wheele of Deskes wch at this tyme standes there) shall remayne still in those place As alsoe the marble table sonne dyall and pictures wch I have placed in the Garden of all wch I desyre an Inventorie may be made by sure Register and the things to contynue alwayes in the House as they are.

Item I give to my Daughter *Harvye* all the furniture wch is usuallye in that Chamber wch wee cal the Flannell Chamber and in the ynner Chamber thereof.

Item I give to the Poore of the parish of S^t. Gregories where I dwell Five pounds. And to the Poore of eache of the Parrishes of S^t. Dunstans in the West London & of Seavenoakes in Kent and of Blunham in Bedfordshire To eache parish Twentye poundes.

Item I give to the Right Hono^rable the *Earle of Kent* Patron of that Churche of Blunham the Picture of layinge Christe in the Tombe wch hangs in my Study.

Item my Will is that all the former Legacies given in monye be payde within six weekes after my deathe. All which Legacies beinge soe payed and all charge that can in

any waye fall uppon my Executors being discharged, my
Will is That my plate & bookes (such bookes only beinge
excepted as by a Schedule signde wth my hand I shall give
awaye) and all my other goods beinge praysde and soulde
all my Poore Estate of money left & money soe raised &
money lent maye be distributed in manner and forme
following.

Firste I will that for the mayntenance of my dearly
beloved Mother whome it hathe pleased God after a plenti-
full Fortune in her former tymes to bringe in decaye in her
very olde age, there be ymployed Five hundred poundes of
wch my meaninge is not that the Propertye but only the
proffite shoulde accrue to her during her natural life and after
her deathe the sayd Five hundred poundes to be divided
amongste those my children wch shall be then alive And
because there maye be some tyme before any proffitt of that
monye will come to her handes my will is that Twenty
poundes be payde unto her order and besydes the benefitte
of the Five hundred pounds at the breakinge up of my
familye & her removinge from thence.

Item my Will is that my children's portions shoulde be
equall yf they be unmarried at my deathe But if they be
marryed before, they are to content themselves wth that w^ch
they shall have received from me at theire marriage Except
I make some other declaration of my Will by a Codicill
hereafter to be annexed my will neverthelesse is that my
eldest daughter *Constance Harvye* whoe receyved from me
at her firste marriadge but Fyve hundred poundes for
portion shal be equall wth the rest whoe at my deathe are
to receive portions though theire portions amounte to noe
more than Five hundred poundes.

And therefore whereas there is at this tyme in my handes
a conveighance of a certaine Farme calld the Tannhouse
from her husband *M^r. Samuel Harvye* in consideracon of
Twoe hundred and fiftye poundes payde by me for his use
in wch there is a Provisoe for redemption for a certaine
tyme. My will is that if that Twoe hundred and fiftie
poundes be accordinglie payde it be then added to the whole
Stocke wch is to be devided amongste the children If for
defaulte of payment it become absolutelie myne my will is
that that land be reassured unto him and his heires w^th

this condicon & not oth'wise that it be added to her Joynture for hir lief if shee survive him and if it fall oute
that this land be thus given backe, whereby my Daughter
received Twoe hundred and fiftie poundes above hir former
Five hundred, my will is that shee make noe clayme to any
parte of my state by any thinge formerlye sayd in this my
Will till all the rest of my children have received Seaven
hundred & fiftie poundes because upon the whole matter
shee hathe receyved so muche, yf I give backe that land.
But if by Gods goodnes theire portions come to more, Then
shee is alsoe to enter for an equall $p$te of the surplusage
as well in that wch returnes to the children after my
mothers deathe as any othere waye   In all wch accrues w^{ch}
may come to my Daughter *Harvye* my will is that uppon
receipt thereof her husband make a proportionable addicon
to her Joynture in land or els that that monye wch shall
soe accrue unto them maye come to the longer liver of them.

Item I give to my sonne *George* that Annuyte of Fortye
pounds yearelie for the payment of wch my hono'able frend
S^r. John Dãvers of Chelsey Knighte hathe some yeares since
accepted from me Firste Twoe hundred poundes and after
One hundred marcks of wch Annuyte thoughe there be as
yett noe assurance made, yett there remayne wth me Bondes
for those sevrall sommes   And *S^r. John Dãvers* will uppon
requeste made, either make suche assurance or repaye the
moneye as he hathe alwayes promisd me   And my will is
that whatsov^r aryses to my other children my sonne George
be made equall to them that Two hundred poundes and
one hundred marcks beinge accounted as part of the Somme.

Item my will is that the portions wch shall become due
to my twoe Sonnes *John* & *George* & to my eldest daughter
Bridgett yett unmarryed be payed to them as soone after
my deathe as may be because they are of years to governe
theire portions.   But for my twoe younger daughters *Margaret*
and *Elizabeth* my will is that theire portions be payde at the
dayes of theire severall marriages or at theire age of Twoe
and Twentye yeares, theire portions to be ymployed in the
meane tyme for theire mayntenance and for the increase of
y^{eir} portions if it will beare it.   And if they or either of
them dye before that tyme of marriage or of twoe and
twentye yeares that then the portions of them or either of

them soe dyenge shal be equallye devided amongste my
othere children wch shal be alyve at theire deathe   And
because there maye be some tyme before they receave any-
thinge for theire mayntenance oute of the ymployment of
theire portions, my Will is that to eache of my children
John, George, Bridgett, Margarett and *Elizabeth* there be
Twentye poundes payde at the same tyme as I have formerlie
appointed the like somme to be payde to my Mother.

Item I give to my hono'able and faithful friendes *Mr
Robert Karr* of his Mjst^{ye} bedchamb^r that Picture of mine
wch is taken in Shaddowes and was made very many years
before I was of this Profession   And to my hono'able frend
Sr John Danvers I give what Picture he shall accept of
those that remayne unbequeathed.

And this my last Will and Testament made in the feare
of God whose Mercye I humbly begge & constantlye relye
uppon in Christe Jesus & in perfecte love & charitie wth all
the Worlde whose pardon I aske from the lowest of my
Servants to the highest of my Superior^s.   I writt all wth
myne owne hand & subscribed my name to everie page
thereof of wch there are five & sealled the same & published
and declared it to be my last Will the thirteenth daye of
December 1630 ——

J DONNE —— in the pr^{ce} of ——

SAMUEL HARVYE —— EDW PICKERELL ——
JOHN HARRINGTON —— JOHN GIBBS ——
ROBERT CHRISTMASS.

(This Will was proved 5th April 1631 by Dr Henry
Kinge, and Dr John Montford, the Executors.)

INDEX

233

Vincent, Donne's coachman, App. C.

WALTON, Izaak, biographer of Donne, 109 and *passim*.
—— his near neighbour at St. Dunstan's, 166.
—— watches his dying-bed, 218.
—— Izaak, the younger, 217.
Weldon, 51.
White, Francis, Dean of Carlisle, 187.
—— Thomas, Dr., 162.
Whitehall, 112.

Willoughby, Lord, 35.
Williams, John, Bishop of Lincoln, 183.
Wilt Thou forgive that sin where I begun, 206.
Winniffe, Dr. Thomas, Donne's successor as Dean, 133, 216, App. C.
Winwood, Ralph, secretary, 122.
Wooley, Sir Francis, of Pyrford, 16, 21, 59.
Wotton, Sir Henry, 11, 86, 87.

YORK HOUSE, 31.

PRINTED BY
MORRISON AND GIBB LIMITED, EDINBURGH.